# Rapture

# Rapture

Gail Glode

Parchment Global Publishing
100 South Juniper St.
Philadelphia, PA 19107
www.parchmentglobalpublishing.com

ISBN: 978-1-952302-68-8 (sc)
ISBN: 978-1-952302-69-5 (e)

Library of Congress Control Number: 2021922017

Also by Gail Glode:

Peace in Your Heart
Thank God for Red Shoes
Starring You

To the indimenticabile, unforgettable, people of Italy, whom I love with all my heart...welcoming, open, generous, sensitive, with an exquisite and incomparable language, uniquely expressive and evocative, and hearts of pure gold - di oro puro.

To Amy, Benji, Melanie and Tim - for a world of wonder and love without bounds.

To Maurice, Jean-Marc, Denise, Diane, Martine and Marie and to all of my Québécoise family, who always loved me and treated me with acceptance in spite of my differences.

To my British ancestry, from whom I learned a love of cabbage roses, tea on tiered plates and an absolutely fervent passion for reading, fostered by Pookie and Noddy, and a million other beautiful English books.

For all my beloved friends, my family really, in Abruzzo, who have taught me how to live, and have made me feel loved - cherished - like never before.

To Alessandro, my incredible friend and kindred spirit - I have no words to express my immense gratitude for your being in my life. Baci, b.b.

Lascia che me tuffi
nella tua anima di acqua
e insieme vaghiamo
per le isole dell'infanzia

Ugo Stefanutti
da Citta Dondolante


Allow me to dip
into your watery soul
and, together, we will wander
to the islands of our childhood

Ugo Stefanutti
from The Swaying City

La Serenissima

Enigma

She administers her silence like no other,
a tongue she has spoken
for thousands of years.

He often feels like
a well-lubricated ghost before her,
possessing her, yet not her silent thoughts,
wondering how she populates the deserts
of her silence when she feels his seed
forgotten by him,
and whom she smiles to
as she stares right past him.

She looks at him with a mixture
of boredom, wisdom, and weariness.
Her gaze is neither elusive nor sustained
neither inquisitive nor indifferent:
how many generations of women
are needed to achieve that gaze
as penetrating as a steel blade
born from a long genetic memory
of untold lives spent as prey
in dark holds of ships, her thighs bloody
among burning ruins and bodies,
weaving and unweaving her cloth
across infinite winters.

How often has he sensed the presence
of thousands upon thousands of them
behind this woman's steady presence
in every corner of his life.
He envies her free love
a love no prize-conditioned
for she's as pure as a theorem
as dense as a black star.

Deep down he sees her armed
with all the weapons god and nature
have granted woman to defend herself.


Yet undaunted,
Enigma

the intemperate pride bred in his blood
ordains his desire to penetrate her
to become her watchmaker
to examine her in her sleep
to snatch the secret cogwheels
to discover her between ticks.

Though he often thinks
himself her lover, in the end
he must confess
he's merely her witness.


Diego Bastianutti
from "The Bloody Thorn"

This book has a soundtrack...at the beginning of each chapter, sometimes within, and, sometimes, at the end of a chapter. If you have the songs on CD or an MP3 player, great. If not, consider YouTube or something of that nature. Or, better yet and if you can, go and buy the songs that touch you and, in doing so, support the artists, the songwriters and everyone involved in the production of these masterpieces that bring so much pleasure to the world. These people, and so many others, have their finger in the socket of the Source.

# Capitolo Uno

Listen to "This Is It" by Kenny Loggins and Michael McDonald

"Oh, my God! We're here..."

Fifty shades of gray, literally. Charcoal and silver, rainbow clouds and shot silk, slate and smoke, pearl and mother-of-pearl. Stardust and turtledove, foggy dawn and white gold, pewter and spilled ink. As the plane approached the Marco Polo Airport, Margaret began to feel that sense of well-being, of pure delight creeping through all her veins, that sense of excitement, of anticipation. Water and light and sea and sky.

And the palest, most-identifiable-as-uniquely-Venetian colour in the world. Water colour. What was the colour? Blue? Or was it some other colour - a colour, as yet, unnamed? Was it even a colour? Celestial. Muted. Vibrant. Soft. Embracing. Delicate. Etheric. Wispy. As if it could tear in an instant. A symphony really, full of crescendos and nuances both.

And then, as Margaret exited the airport, that first magnificent intake of Venetian air. Full of moisture but not humid; warm, and cool at the same time; soft, silky. And, in marked contrast, the utter craziness of the airport traffic.

Margaret was back in Venice, a place that, quite literally, made her heart sing, a place she had loved for almost thirty-five years. All those years ago, she had come to Venice as a young woman to study the Italian language and to learn about the Italian culture. It had been a summer school course, only six weeks, but what a six weeks it had been. The experience truly had been life-altering...no exaggeration.

Margaret had been born in Quebec City and had grown up in a bilingual family...English and French. Even her name reflected it. Margaret, very British - Aimée, very French - Gabriel, very bilingual. When, as an adult, Margaret had started to learn Italian, it had been relatively easy for her because, as she told people in Italy, she had already had French "nel cuore mio" - in her heart, in her blood.

Her father was Québécois and her mother had been born in England, and, most fortunate of girls, Margaret had been brought up bilingual. Together, her parents had given her the best of both cultures - tradition and joie de vivre; a love of reading and a natural tendency to sing and to dance; roast beef and Yorkshire pudding and tourtière; rosy apples on scrubbed wooden tables and the indescribable importance of the love of family.

She considered herself fortunate and blessed to have grown up in such an environment, having been given the opportunity for the first-hand appreciation for two cultures - for two solitudes. It had formed her.

Margaret had never been the same since that summer school course in Venice, smitten by the city - without its blasted tourists, mind you. Touched by the warmth, the passion, the intensity and the - what was the right word? - the sheer generosity of spirit of the Italian people, Margaret knew that the trip had changed her life forever. It wasn't perfect, this complex, intriguing society, but it was perfect for her.

Venice had fit her like a very elegant, form-fitting, silk evening glove - sophisticated, simple, complicated - all of a turn. In Venice, the city of masks, ironically, she had dropped hers. Venice had sculpted her, chipping away the surplus and revealing her authentic - her naked - her Italian - self.

As an adult, Margaret had moved from Quebec to attend university. For a whole host of reasons, she had never really felt in the right skin - nella pelle giusta – in her Anglo-Saxon environment in Canada, as much as she loved the country itself. And she did love it.

She often said that if, in previous lives, a person had been very, very good - exceptionally good - they got to come back the next time and live in Canada. It was an amazingly great place and she felt privileged to live there.

And to have brought up a family there. She, and her former husband, had brought up four incredible children - each one of them perfect in her or his own way. Now, they were spread all over the globe, with families of their own, lives of their own.

For a while now, it had been time for Margaret to pick up her own life... never easy, after having a vocation for a couple of decades. To find oneself trying to remember what it is that used to make life worth living before that all-important, all-encompassing family. She was sixty - just - but sixty nonetheless. A big number. A wacky number. She didn't feel sixty. But she was, even though, inside, well...that was an entirely different matter. Sometimes she'd catch sight of herself reflected in a store window or something and think, "Who the hell is that?" Not an unusual reaction for a person of her age.

Margaret had four grown children...each so different, one from the next, and she loved each one, had an entirely different relationship with each one, but loved them the way she loved no one else.

But, just as you could love more than one person, Margaret loved the many faces of a few different places. Venezia, however, had been her first and, she had to admit, her favourite, lover. Being there was perpetually like those first few sensations of infatuation. It made her feel inexplicably happy, giddy at moments, giving everyone who saw her the impression that she was irrepressibly in love with life. She walked differently, with an extra little swivel to her hips. She immediately started using her hands more - an intrinsic extension of her voice - inexorably linked - as if they were connected directly to her vocal chords, to the muscles in her face. Together, an orchestra of communication.

Margaret stopped, completely still, closed her eyes, drank it in - had a moment. This always happened to her in Venice. Wordless moments - moments that she just wanted to bottle. Moments to keep in a bottle, so she could take a swig whenever she felt the need. To describe it as "bliss" felt trite. It was a wordless thing. Wordless. To try to describe it was simply not possible. It couldn't be voiced.

For some reason, it reminded her of a story that she had heard about the Etruscans, one of the ancient peoples of Italy, and their tears. They, apparently, had had a tradition of collecting all the tears they shed and infusing them with rose petals. That infusion was given only to the closest people in that person's life, a priceless gift of the true and essential essence of the giver...the true elixir of one's soul, one's "anima" as they said in Italian.

Oh, those Etruscans... They were something else...

That story always made her feel touched, to the point of dropping a tear, so beautiful a sentiment, a little bittersweet. Somehow that wordless, indescribable thing she had been trying to capture had a bit of that bittersweetness in it too. Touched to the point of tears. She kept wanting to learn more about those amazing people, who just intrigued her, but there was very little known about them. Maybe this time she'd find out more.

Once, a couple of years ago, in the Etruscan Museum in Tuscany, Margaret had marveled at the perfect miniature duck, made of gold, part of a piece of jewelry, but, most of all, at a beautiful sculptured funeral urn, the perfect replica of the young woman's charming and - what was the most surprising and amazing - smiling face. The sweetest smile.

This time, Margaret was to be in Italy for three months - partly, for the sheer pleasure of it, and partly, a pivotal business trip. Margaret had never been there for that long before. It was mid-September and she would be in Italy until just before Christmas.

The pleasure part was easy. Venice was going to be her base, her home once more. For three whole months... She hadn't been back for more than a year. She was going to walk and read and write and walk some more and paint and see her favourite churches and walk some more. She was going to admire the sky and the sea and venture into the lagoon and deliberately try to get lost in the Venetian labyrinth, although she'd discovered long ago and many times over that getting lost in Venice was impossible. All the street corners said "Per Rialto', the Rialto Bridge, halfway down the Gran Canale; or "Per San Marco", for Piazza San Marco, the heart of the city; or "Ferrovia", the train station, directing people back to the main points of reference in the city.

The business part was altogether something else. The next day, Diana, her friend - and now, her agent as well - was arriving from Vancouver. For as long as Margaret could remember, everyone had always called Diana "Di", just like Princess Di. Di and Margaret enjoyed one another's company very much and always laughed a lot, always a good thing. For tonight and perhaps the next night, Margaret was staying at her favourite hotel, the locanda (inn in English) where she had stayed, on and off, for more than a quarter of a century. And then, tomorrow, when Di arrived, or perhaps the next day, depending on how Di felt, they would move into their apartment. She'd never had an apartment in Venice before and she was really relishing it.

Here and there throughout the next few months, she and Di were going to promote Margaret's book, "Thank God for Red Shoes." They had tried to concentrate all the publicity outings together so that the work part and the pleasure part could be separated somewhat, but it just hadn't worked out that way. There were a few book signings; a couple of interviews, one pretty big; and at least one public-speaking engagement confirmed.

It was so strange how things worked sometimes. Margaret had written the book - actually, in truth, the book had written itself - several years ago. For the entire month of January, she had awakened at 3:30 or 4:00 a.m. virtually every day. Ideas had swirled in her head. In an attempt to go back to sleep, she had meditated, first working her way through her chakras and opening herself to the universe, and then finding the balance point between feeling grounded through her root chakra and feeling connected to Spirit through her crown chakra. Margaret had learned much about this - meditation, channelling, Spirit – since she had moved to her Gulf Island home in the Pacific, an island which was said to be a gigantic crystal, amplifying everyone's intuitive abilities.

During those early morning sessions, much of the information that had come through had come almost like dictation. For Margaret heard things. She had been given the gift...some would have said she was fey. She heard things, and she saw things. Clairaudient. Clairvoyant. And most of all, she had been given the gift of sometimes just, out of the blue, knowing things. Clairsentient.

That January, Margaret had written and written and written, taking down all the ideas that had come to her. Sometimes she had thought it was done for a particular session or section and she had turned turn out the light to go back to sleep, and then, unbelievably, it actually begun again. And Margaret had had to turn the light back on and write the rest of it. She had taken to keeping pen and paper by her bed, the only sensible thing to do.

Sometimes, instead of almost dictation, the information had come as some kind of riddle, a riddle she had then feel compelled to follow to its conclusion, to solve. Margaret had a trunk full of notebooks, filled with such information...a huge trunk full.

When it had come to the information about a new understanding of "ego", she had tried to send the manuscript to May Publishing, probably the most well-respected publisher in the area of things spiritual, but they had, very kindly, but also very firmly, responded that they did not accept unsolicited manuscripts and advised her to find a literary agent. A friend in the publishing world had told her that that was a bunch of garbage and that she should think about self-publishing. In the end, she had done exactly that, with the help of a very talented designer and a printing company in Victoria.

But, during one of Margaret's trips to Italy, her dearest Italian friend, Elisabetta, had wanted to read the book. Things seemed to get surreal from that point on. "It is just remarkable..." Elisabetta had said. "Really ground-breaking! We need to have this book in Italy. We must have it. We have to do it." Elisabetta had a friend who knew a publisher. Elisabetta, a native Venetian, had translated the book herself, working with Margaret to ensure that every connotation, every concept was as intended. And then, all hell - or heaven, really - had broken loose.

It was as if the book had taken on a life of its own. What had seemed so difficult - so absolutely unlikely - suddenly had become supremely easy. It wasn't without its hitches, but, like Venice herself, it did have that odd and old sense of strangely beautiful magic about it. La Serenissima, "The Most Serene", as the city was known, was decrepit, ephemeral. Hopefully, the book would not be. Venice had endured. Hopefully, the book would also endure.

It seemed that sometimes this fascinating and intriguing phenomenon kicked in. It had happened with "The Bold and the Beautiful", a day-time TV show produced in California and in English, in the original version. In Italy, with Italian dubbed in for the voices of Brooke Logan and Ridge Forrester and all the characters, "Beautiful" - pronounced "Bee-ooo-tee-fool" in Italy - had become one of the most successful and beloved programs on Italian television. The show was about the fashion industry and that certainly hadn't hurt. And, of course, it was populated by very beautiful, truly gorgeous people.

At one point there was a rumour that Susan Flannery, who played the magnificent matriarch on the show, was going to leave the show. People in Italy were beyond distraught. Susan's character often would say, with great disgust, "For heaven's sake...." and it translated perfectly, "Per l'amore del cielo..." She could have been from Milan or Rome, no problem.

Ron Moss, who played Ridge Forrester, was, and still is - there's no other word for it - a demi-god. He had come and done "Ballando Sotto Le Stelle", the Italian "Dancing With The Stars", and won!!!! He was Adonis and he was adored, chiseled jaw and gorgeous muscles all.

Well, in any case, this quirky phenomenon had kind of happened with Margaret's book too. One thing had led into something else, and then something else. The book had become relatively successful - but a little controversial - in Italy, although, in Canada, and certainly in the U.S. and elsewhere in the world, it was virtually unheard of.

Elisabetta really had been at the bottom of it all and it had been her contacts that had made the whole thing possible. Rather suddenly, Margaret had needed an agent, a publicist, to help organize it all. And who else but her friend, Di, who had always been a staunch supporter - who had supreme faith in her and her ability to channel.

Margaret had been working in Canada as a designer on a contract basis and when the funding had dried up, quite suddenly, she'd become available to spend the time in Italy to promote her book. The universe just worked that way sometimes. The abrupt ending to her contract had been challenging, for a whole variety of reasons. But, as they say, "When one door closes..."

Di would be there the next day. In the meantime, Margaret needed to get from Mestre, on the mainland, where the airport was, down into Venice proper.

Usually she travelled light. This time, she had a bit more with her since she was staying for a longer period of time. Venice was not a great city to be walking around with a suitcase on wheels. Cobbled streets and a million bridges – what could be worse that making that horrific racket as one tried to navigate the city?

She climbed onto the bus going to Piazzale Roma. "Buon giorno, Signore. Va alla ferrovia?" she checked. She'd ended up on the wrong bus or train too often – had developed the habit of asking several times, even after all those years. "Sì, sì, Signora," answered the bus driver.

On to Piazzale Roma, where everyone had to leave their cars. Then a short walk over the bridge to the Ferrovia, the railway station, and from there, on to the best leg of the voyage - the fantastic ride on a vaporetto, a water bus, all the way down the Gran Canale. It never failed to thrill her - in spite of the lack of sleep on the long flight from Vancouver. Palazzos, geraniums, gondolas, all welcoming her back - embracing her - enfolding her into the heart of the city.

She just loved it. Loved it. A guy yacking away on his cell phone while he guided his beautiful wooden boat, no hands, down the canal. Margaret grinned. The unexpected gardens punctuating the incredible buildings, some with those distinctive gothic windows, buildings which were feeling, unfortunately, more and more like a movie set, as though there were nothing at all behind those incredible facades. People standing in the gondolas that cross the canale in spots where there are no convenient bridges, the cheapest gondola ride in town, by far.

And then, off the vaporetto at San Zaccaria, and threading her way along the crazy way back to the hotel - a crazy kind of Gretyl, following metaphorical pigeon-dropping crumbs along the unlikely way home.

And then to the Albergo del Rimedio - ah, home - up the million stairs to Sandra's broad smile and double-cheeked kisses with a resounding, "Ben tornata!!!! Welcome back!!!! Com'è stato il viaggio stavolta? How was the trip this time? Ti posso offrire qualcosa...sugo di arancia, un caffè? Would you like something...orange juice or coffee?"

"No, grazie, tesoro. Sono stanca da morire. No, thank you, darling. I'm dead tired."

And after chatting and catching up with Sandra a few more minutes, up more stairs to her favourite room, number 19. When she had first met Sandra, Margaret had been twenty-six and Sandra had been sixteen. Now, all this time later, Sandra had inherited the hotel, which was essentially the same except for some beautiful renovations, updated plumbing, air conditioning and the like.

Her favourite room was quite small and opened out onto rooftops and church steeples and bell towers. A veritable sea of terra cotta tiles. Waves - "onde", they said in Italy - of them. And incredible rooftop gardens, with such stunning greenery and flowers everywhere - the geranium of course, but other things too, clusters of flowers she didn't recognize, some of them the most unbelievable celestial blue. And there, over in the corner, the dome of the Basilica itself...

And, finally, onto her bed. Always the best part - looking up at her Venetian ceiling - always with some disbelief that she was really there. The church bells started. Scores of them. They all went off at different times...the strangest thing. Charming, somehow.

Exhausted, Margaret fell into the deepest sleep, dozing soundly on and off for twelve hours, waking only occasionally and briefly to reassure herself that both she and the city itself were really there. It was still dark out. She somehow never quite believed that Venice really was there, right outside her window, that it actually existed. That she hadn't just dreamt the whole thing.

Back to sleep, smiling.

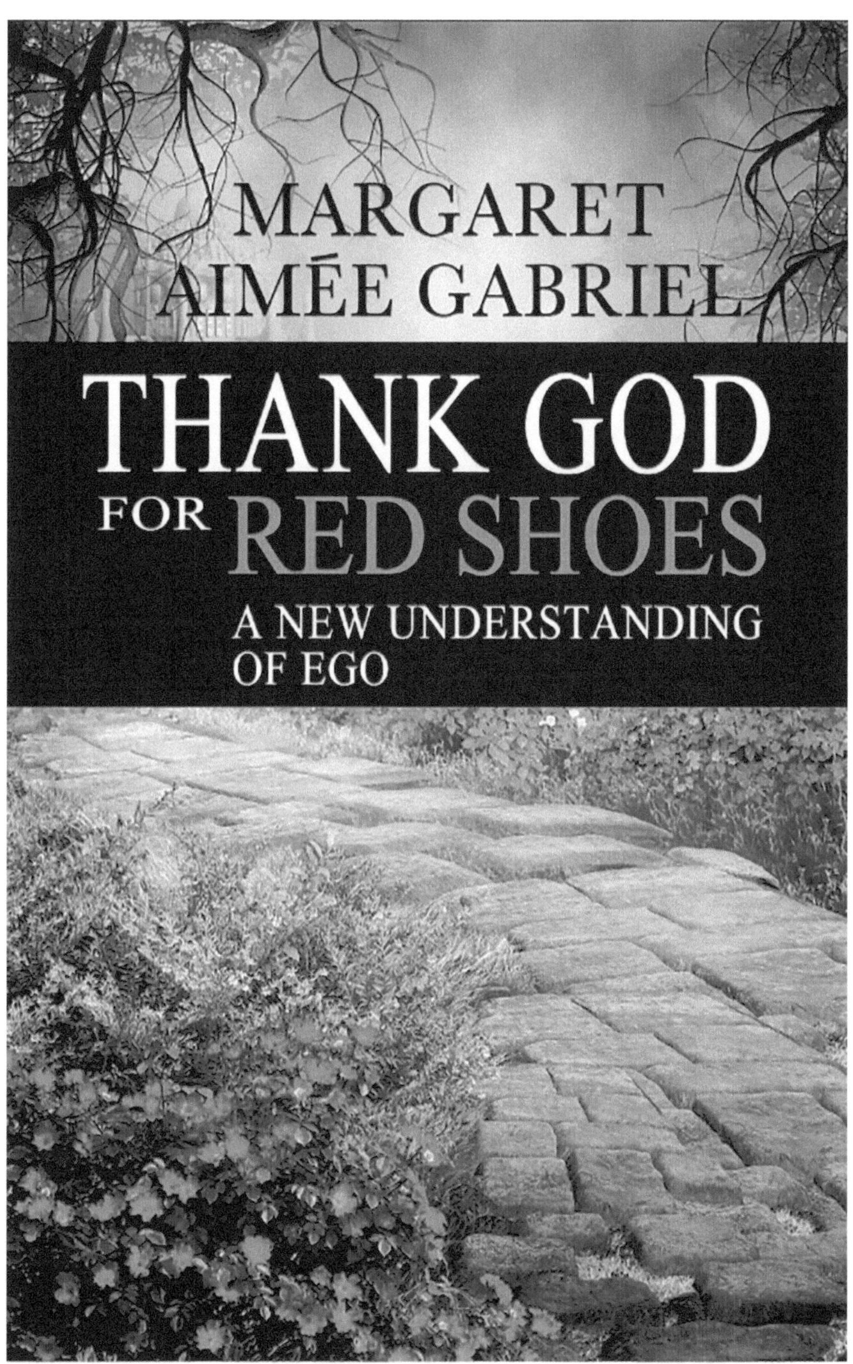

MARGARET AIMÉE GABRIEL
THANK GOD FOR RED SHOES
A NEW UNDERSTANDING OF EGO

Poor old ego. It's always being bashed.

So, why do we do that?

Is it possible that we have misunderstood it?

Is there another plausible explanation of ego which might
make better sense of this powerful internal mechanism?

Furthermore, is there a possibility that this new
understanding would offer us the chance to
change the way we look at the world?

The answer - to all three questions?

Yes. Yes. And yes.

There is.

There absolutely is.

To Victoria, Elizabeth, Garnett and Stanhope

# *Table of Contents*

# Thank God for Red Shoes

## Chapter 1 - Ruby Slippers for the Journey

Journeys. Wondrous, wondrous journeys.

Like Dorothy in the Wizard of Oz, we all experience, learn, grow and evolve on our journey down the yellow brick road. Her red shoes, her ruby slippers, are magical - they ground her but they also allow her to soar home, this place that she's taken for granted. Our lives are like that. So precious, so utterly precious but, for a whole host of reasons, we sometimes take those lives for granted. Or we get it, but, unfortunately, just before we perish, and have missed the boat about truly living our lives basking in this priceless wisdom.

As in many myths and legends from around the world and across the ages, the journey on the outside is a metaphor for the journey within. The learning through relationships and circumstances is a metaphor for self-discovery.

Santiago, the shepherd boy in Paulo Coelho's "The Alchemist", goes on an incredible voyage of self-discovery. Harry Potter learns about good and evil, with all its twists and turns. Oedipus Rex discovers the greatest form of suffering, the unspeakable tragedy of self-loathing. In Milton's "Paradise Lost", we learn, "The mind is its own place and in itself can make a hell of heaven and a heaven of hell." (1)

While on the journey, we experience our greatest highs and lows, our greatest loves and our greatest fears. We experience wonder, immense joy, moments of inspiration, moments of bliss and we also experience moments of anger, of sadness and sorrow, of frustration, of disappointment and despair...of fear, in all its faces. Often, we are confronted by our deepest fears and demons and learn to reflect on how we dealt with them.

Sometimes our obstacles seem to overwhelm us. We get mired in the day-to-day. We start to accept the negative as the truth and to believe there is no way out.

All the while, it's the Universe telling us that we're on the wrong track - time to do and be something different.

Other times, we have an "AHA" moment, or, indeed, a series of them - moments when we understand, profoundly, that what we were searching for is right there inside of us and has been all along.

The Universe is nodding its head in encouragement. It is an indication of the moveable feast of self-realization and self-love.

We've recognized who we really are - at our core, and eternally, Spirit, and yet, simultaneously but temporarily, personalities with unique gifts to share to contribute to making the world a better place.

We experience the benefits of contrast. We understand the intrinsic underlying purpose of duality and that is, quite simply but utterly elegantly, experience. It is the ability of the Universe to experience itself.

We are one but we are not the same. We are made of the same stuff but we are not identical. Our Spirit is all one – our personalities are unique.

We learn an essential truth.

Yes, we are in the world, but, more importantly, the world is in us. The potential for good and evil is within each and every one of us. There are not some of us who are exclusively good and some of us who are exclusively evil.

Our lack of recognition of this potential within each individual one of us continues to allow us to project our unresolved fears and our own potential for evil onto others.

Traditionally, we have battled this evil. We believed we had to fight it. Tooth and nail. Our stories are full of it. Our world is full of it. We are full of it.

But the one thing the demon of evil cannot tolerate is compassion. We need to convince our own dark voices of fear that we will not succumb to them and that we will use strong gentleness and non-violence and love to deal with them.

And then, as we begin to truly understand all this and actually live it in our everyday lives, we heal ourselves, one at a time.

We keep putting one foot in front of the other till we wake one day to discover that we are walking our talk. Skipping down the road. Easing on down the road.

We evolve steadfastly, thankful for our very essential defense mechanisms and reassuring our fears, just the way a loving parent does, sometimes with gentle love, sometimes with tough love, always with enduring love, love and more love.

We need to feel grounded. We need to feel love and acceptance. Self-love and self-acceptance. Self-approval. Along the way, we recognize we have magical powers, the power of Spirit.

And, then, we can offer those magical things to others.

And, so, rejoice! What a journey! Peace is at hand. Hallelujah!

And thank God for red shoes.

# Capitolo Due

Listen to "Una Come Te" by Cesare Cremonini

In the morning, Margaret was ready to go. She had flung open her shutters, drinking in the steam rising from the terra cotta roofs, and glimpses of many, many bell towers. Cherry-coloured geraniums and pale, fragile silk sky, full of scalloped marine clouds. After a long, hot shower and after drinking in, in great gulps, the views from her window, she went down to the breakfast room.

"Ciao, Margherita. Hai dormito bene? Morning, Margaret. Did you sleep well?" asked Sandra.

"Sì, sì, ho dormito bene, come sempre. Yes, yes, I slept very well, as always," she responded with real bounce in her voice. "After breakfast, I am going to see Maria down at the bar."

"Oh, Maria... she has not been well you know."

"Something serious...?" asked Margaret.

"No, no, I don't think so."

"Signora Margherita !" she heard with a great squeal of joy as she entered the breakfast room. It was Caterina who had worked at the albergo for quite a long while. She and Margaret had always had good chemistry, right from the very first time they had met one another and Caterina was always delighted to see her, which didn't happen often enough.

"Caterina, ciao, ciao, tutto bene? Hi, hi Caterina, is everything well?"

"Sì sì." They kissed one another's cheeks.

"Caffè, cappuccino, caffè latte, cosa prende? What can I get you?" asked Caterina. Margaret could hardly eat. But coffee - that was different - and a glass of spremuta, freshly-squeezed orange juice. Ahh, that first sip of Italian coffee was always the best...there was nothing like it. Nothing. On the buffet, there was yogurt and cheese and prosciutto and fruit, but all Margaret could eat was a bit of her cornetto, a buttery croissant filled with Italian apricot jam.

"Una bella giornata davvero. A truly beautiful day," said Caterina, beaming her magnificent smile.

"You're right, Caterina" Margaret answered in Italian. "I am going to the bar to see Maria and then, I don't know what will be next... My friend, Diana, isn't coming till later today, so I might just go for a walk." Margaret pronounced Di's name the Italian way, "Dee-an-na."

Margaret continued, "That, and sleep some more to get over this crazy time change - fuso orario. I always find it so hard this way, from Canada to Europe."

"Yes, everybody says it is much worse this way that the return way," commiserated Caterina.

After breakfast Margaret dropped off her key at the desk and, as she went down the stairs to the ground level, she caught sight of herself reflected in the glass doors. She really did look better. She did.

Margaret had struggled with her weight almost her whole life...at least, from the time she first went to school. She had been on her first serious diet when she was sixteen, and with her help of her family doctor and his prescription for diet pills, she had lost a lot of weight. That was the beginning of the pattern, the pattern that so many have experienced.

From that point on, she had gone up and down and up and down, at what turned out to be perfect ten-year intervals, and happened to coincide with Oprah's weight losses also. Each time, as the weight came back on, her weight had gone up and up - the well-known yo-yo effect. Finally, she had had to decide that she had to just live with it. She had dieted herself into obesity.

But, all that had started to change. From the time that she had spent a month in Italy a while back, and from the time that she had allowed herself to do what really made her heart soar, the weight had, quite magically, started to fall away. She had found herself listening to her body, eating only exactly what she wanted, in exactly the amount she wanted. She no longer ate in front of the TV. Every mouthful made her declare how absolutely delicious it was. Maybe that had been a real key. To eat with absolute, abandoned pleasure and delight. Never, never - but never - out of sadness or loneliness or boredom. Or distractedly. The end result was a much trimmer Margaret. Not thin. Not yet. But thinner. And infinitely happier.

After breakfast, Margaret fairly ran to the Bar La Serenissima.

"Ciao, ciao, Maurizio! Hi, hi Maurizio? Come stai? Bene? How are you? Well?" she greeted her old friend at the bar. Maurizio had worked at the bar forever. He had been there when Margaret had been a young woman and he was there still.

"Margherita, ma che meraviglia sei diventata! Ciao, amore, ciao. Margaret, what a wonder you have become. Hello, love, hello. Ben tornata! Welcome back!!"

"La Signora Maria, c'è? Is Signora Maria here?"

"Sì, sì, certo. La vado a cercare. Un attimo... Yes, yes, of course. I'll go find her. Just a moment... Maria!"

"Signora Maria! Sono io, Margherita. It's me, Margaret. Come stai? How are you? Tutt'a posto? Is everything all right?"

"Ohe, Margherita, non ti ho vista da tanto tempo. Sì, tesoro, come diciamo, tutt'a posto, ma niente in ordine. Ehi, Margaret, I haven't seen you for so long. Yes, darling, as we say, everything in its place, but nothing in order."

Signora Maria did not look well. She had aged so much... But what could one expect? It was true, she was getting on. Margaret had first met her on that first visit, thirty-five years ago. She and her classmates, and, often, their professor, had taken to walking to the bar every evening after dinner to have a coffee. At first, Signora Maria had scared her to death. Teeny and tough, never cracking a smile, she had seemed like a tiny, ferocious Venetian witch, like befana, the little witch doll that hung in some Italian kitchens. Hard. Inscrutable. Terse.

But, she'd mellowed over the month and a half, as they got to know one another. And, just before Margaret had left, to return to Canada, she had gone to the florist, one of several thousand in the city, it seemed. She had visited the amazing florist that she had discovered one day on the way to their classroom, and had bought a bouquet - an incredible bouquet - of flowers to say thank you and goodbye - no, not goodbye, but, "arrivederci", until we see one another again – to Signora Maria. They had cried, both of them. Both of them.

Every time Margaret visited Venice, one of the first things she did was to go see Signora Maria. And, every time she did, they'd pick up where they'd left off. Margaret wasn't sure how old Signora Maria was. When Margaret had first met her, Maria might have been forty or so, although she seemed much older. That would make her about seventy-five now. Signora Maria was from Milan, originally, but had married a Venetian and had lived in Venice virtually all of her adult life. Running the bar was challenging. People and taxes and rising prices and either too many tourists at once or too few, and expensive supplies in a city that was sometimes challenging to access, even though they'd done very well over the centuries.

But, this time, Signora Maria really looked haggard. Margaret had seen her just last year and she had seemed relatively well. There Maria was, year after year, at the bar, plugging away, even after all this time. Once, a million years ago, Maria had wanted to be a soprano. God had given her a voice - a splendid voice.

That dream, however, had had to be put aside once she married and the children had started to come. Once the children were grown, she had tried to join a choir so that she could sing her heart out. But, as for many, if not all, entrepreneurs, the business did not allow her a life. She was at it seven days a week. That's just the way it was. Tough. Very, very tough. And what about singing? The stage? La Scala? Violetta? Manon? All such thoughts had had to be buried. There was a living to be made.

And now, here she was, into her eighties. She had not been feeling well for a long time. Her children kept urging her to go to the doctor, but she didn't like doctors. Not at all. There had been a time when, like many Italian people, she had gone to the doctor at the drop of a hat, for every little thing. But, those days were gone. They hadn't saved Antonio, had they? Her beloved Antonio, bent over in pain. Not one bit...

Margaret and Maria caught up on what news there was. Maria made her a frothy cappuccino, which she offered her every time Margaret went in. Maria hadn't let her pay for a coffee for years. They chatted about what had gone on over the year and a bit since they had seen one another. They always seemed to be able to pick up where they left off. That was such a lovely sensation...

"Allora, devo andarmene. So, I should get going," said Margaret, thinking that she needed to leave herself some time to get up to the airport. "Ciao, ciao e ci vediamo domani. Bye, bye, and we'll see each other tomorrow," said Margaret.

"Se Dio vuole. God willing. Ciao, tesoro, ciao. Bye, darling, bye," answered Signora Maria. A big hug and kisses on the cheeks.

On her short walk back to her hotel, Margaret couldn't help but worry. Signora Maria really didn't seem herself. She really didn't. Thinner. Drawn. Immensely tired. In the strong morning sun, and then in the shade of the Chiesa Santa Maria Formosa, Margaret became aware of a man behind her. She took a quick look over her shoulder. He was a young man, early thirties perhaps, a beautiful face, blond hair and, in his arms, on one side an armful of roses and, on the other...a miniature version of himself. There were a lot of people with fair hair in Venice - leftover Nordic influence, they said.

"Guard' amore. Sono belle, no? Look at them, love. They're beautiful, aren't they?" the man asked his young son. The little boy nodded wildly. "For your Mamma, who is also astoundingly beautiful. Oh, love, they are so beautiful, these roses, that perhaps you'd like to give each of them a kiss. Che ne pensi? What do you think?" And with that, the teeny boy, Dresden doll that he was, started dropping teeny kisses, baci, on each of the roses.

Margaret, who had stopped to let them pass and who had witnessed the exquisite moment, was beside herself. Things like that just touched her foolish, sentimental heart. "Ah, Italy..." she thought. "I've missed you. I really have..."

Later that day, Margaret made her way back up to the Marco Polo airport to collect Di. "You're here!! You're actually here!!" she said, so happily, to Di, who looked just exhausted. Onto the bus to Piazzale Roma, then across the bridge to the front of the train station and onto the vaporetto, the water bus. That whole system of vaporetti was quite incredible, plying up and down the Gran Canale, but also to outer reaches of the port and other islands in the lagoon. "I'm so grateful you're here to take care of me right now, to get me from one place to another." Di had never been to Venice before and suddenly went into rapture, in spite of the impending jet lag. "Oh my lord, it doesn't seem real. There's no place like it in the world. I can see already why you love it so..."

"Oh, you haven't seen anything yet. Wait - just wait - till this place where sea and sky are reflected everywhere, till this water of many different kinds, these bells, these beautiful women and even more beautiful men, the soul of the place – wait till all of that seeps into your bones. Just wait..."

And off they went, down that incredible snaking Gran Canal, one of the most famous snakes in the world. Past Ca' Foscari and Ca' d'oro... and then past the Mercato, the Market, and then immediately under the Rialto Bridge, with its gold shops and millions of tourists. Then onward, under the wooden Accademia Bridge. And then, as the Grand Canal opened up and when they saw Santa Maria della Salute, Di's eyes got even bigger. And then, oh my lord, the Doge's Palace, a pink confection of lace and windows and pillars, of grandeur. And the Piazzetta, leading to Piazza San Marco, with its twin columns of San Marco and San Teodoro...the Campanile, the Bell Tower....the Basilica, in profile.

"Oh, it's just incredible. Is it real?" marveled Di.

Off they got at San Zaccaria, and through another million bodies. How they all got to where they wanted to go, successfully, was a mystery...truly.

As they walked a short distance along Riva degli Schiavoni, the extremely broad pedestrian boulevard that skirted the edge of the city, they couldn't help but laugh at a scene that they had suddenly, al improvviso, come upon.

Walking along, with determination, was a small, bent-over elderly woman, all in black, chasing behind a young man, her grandson perhaps. She was furious. Seriously furious. She had a bucket of water and she kept throwing water at him and swearing at him. "Stronzo che non sei altro. You little piece of shit. Ti butto nel canale. I'll throw you into the canal. Non mi rompere gli coglioni. Don't bust my balls." That vulgar expression was used a fair bit, Margaret had discovered long ago; it always made her laugh; and now made them both laugh, once she had translated for Di. There was something about it that was so preposterous...especially out of the mouth of a sweet little old woman- "che non aveva, che non ha mai avuto, e che non avrà mai" - who didn't have, had never had and would never have - testicles. But it was so funny. And so Italian, somehow.

# Thank God for Red Shoes

## Chapter 2 - Ego-Bashing


Poor old ego. It's always getting bashed. Apparently responsible for all the negative-speak in our minds, it is blamed and shamed for our feeling of separation, our incessant need for approval and outside recognition, our identification with outside things, our need to be right and the cause of a lot of suffering for others and for ourselves. We are told, again and again, that we must battle this. Battle it. Battle it. Battle it. Tame it. Control it. Ignore it. Scorn it. Will it into submission. The nasty thing.

Poor old ego... So, have you ever wondered why ego is like that? I bet you have. It's perplexing, when you really think about it.

Obviously an extremely powerful force in and on us, how does an "egotistical" ego make sense?

Furthermore, if it is that nasty way, why bash it? Bit by bit, many of us are realizing that we have to be for something rather than against it.

Finally, we're starting to understand the big difference between being pro-peace and being anti-war.

Many of us are understanding that we have to be pro-compassion, not anti-violence, that we have to be open-minded rather than right. That we have to be forgiving rather than vengeful. We have to be kind rather than critical. Common sense and every religion in the world, at its core, tells us this.

It is the central point of every major spiritual belief and at the heart of every major religion.

Why, then, do we continue to bash poor old ego?

It's weird. Really weird. There is something about it that doesn't make sense. That doesn't feel right about it.

Something's off. There's got to be something we don't get.

So what is it?

Is it possible that we have actually misunderstood it?

Is there another plausible explanation of ego that makes better sense of this powerful internal mechanism?

Furthermore, is there a possibility that this new understanding would offer us the chance to change the way we look at the world?

The answer - to all three questions.

Yes. Yes. And yes.

There is.

There absolutely is.

# Capitolo Tre

Listen to "Marina", the original song, by Rocco Granata
and to "Marina" by Andre Rieu from his concert in Cortona

The next day, as Di slept for a long while, trying to find her European-time-zone legs, Margaret went to find her old friend, Elisabetta. A few years back, Elisabetta's niece, whom Margaret had met in Canada, had told her that she must look up her aunt who lived in Venice. She thought they would get along very well. And they had. They had, in a very short period of time, become fast friends. In truth, they had become like sisters. Elisabetta was a honey bun. An Italian honey bun. Perhaps with a slightly stiffer shell that her North American counterpart, more doughnut. Elisabetta, however, inside... Well, inside...she was just a pudding heart. Beloved by everyone who knew her.

Margaret used the lion's head door knocker and then there was Elisabetta, popping her head out the window above, her smile as lovely as ever. "Margherita, we've missed you. So much," she exclaimed, in Italian. Elisabetta flew down the stairs to open the door to admit Margaret.

Elisabetta spoke, read and wrote English beautifully; she had been educated in England and her English was impeccable. Nonetheless, she was a Venetian, through and through. She was the one who had translated Margaret's book. They flew into one another's arms...sisters united.

They talked for an hour, mostly about their families, to whom each one of them was devoted. And, a little about men. Or, more precisely, the lack thereof.

"Margaret, I have thinking..." said Elisabetta. "Do you want to come dancing? I go every week and it is really great fun. It is not a great place to meet men, I confess, even though there are many men there. But it a place to have really fantastic fun..."

"What kind of dancing is it?"

"Oh, you know, stuff that old people such as us enjoy. Waltz, and tango, and foxtrot, mazurka, that kind of thing."

"Don't say that! We are not old. Ballroom stuff...that's the kind of dancing you do?"

"Yes, but not much Latin American stuff. The old bones won't take it. Some of the people are in their nineties."

"Really. That always amazes me about here. Lots of people in their eighties and nineties, just carrying on as always."

"Yes, although, mind you, we have our share of ailments - dementia and illness too."

"Yes, sure, I would love to go. I have always loved dancing. It would be fun. I love to dance and I haven't done it for ages. I will come with you. I could use a good time."

"Okay, Saturday at four in the afternoon."

"For an hour or something?"

"No, for three hours, till seven."

"Three hours!? Really? Okay, that sounds like a long time, but I'm up for it..."

"Actually, I could go four times a week, if I wanted to..."

"Four times a week?! And do you?

"Sometimes... It's better than sitting around. I love the music, I see people, and I love to dance. What could be better? You'll see. You'll be converted in no time..."

"Okay, darling, I'm off. Call me. And once we move in, you can come to dinner. Or I can come to you!"

Whenever they got together, Elisabetta and Margaret would spend Saturday nights at Elisabetta's house. They would take turns providing something for dinner, although, in truth, Elisabetta did most of the cooking. Then, like the schoolgirls that they were, they would put on their pajamas and climb into Elisabetta's big bed to watch their favourite television show, one that reunited people, sometimes with happy results, sometimes not so much. Either way, they cried.

And the woman who hosted the show, Adriana Francesca, well, she was amazing...absolutely amazing. She had a real gift as a mediator. Margaret often thought that if they could only get people like Adriana to mediate between conflicting countries, they would be able to solve a lot of the world's chaos. Sit down. Face to face. Look into one another's eyes. Really listen. Have as much time as they needed to express their perspective. Do it all again. And again, if need be.

Elisabetta and Margaret had a few favourite shows, including a singing talent show. The two of them would pick their favourites and root for them, sometimes agreeing, sometimes not. They would cheer and boo and try to predict who was going to win. They were like little kids. Everyone should be so blessed to have such a friend.

The next day, Di and Margaret moved into their apartment. It was adorable. A saccharine word, but that's what it was. Adorable. "Adorabile." Small and, simply-but-beautifully, decorated with all the basics and nothing more. It was in the same neighbourhood as the hotel, so they still could frequent all the same places very easily...the bar, and the pizza spot on the corner, and Margaret's favourite grocery store, not that there were a lot to choose from.

They each settled into their rooms and marvelled at their balcony, overlooking a canal and full of terra cotta pots of geraniums and of cacti. A little lizard raced across the balcony and disappeared over the edge. There was a lovely kitchen plus living room plus dining room; a superb bathroom with both a large shower and - glory be - a large deep tub; and two extremely comfortable bedrooms, each with those stunning tall wooden windows, opening out onto water-colour and pastel views. Rooftops and those crazy rooftop gardens, like wire-surrounded platforms balanced precariously, and miles of terra cotta tiles, and the canal and the superb sky and another view of San Marco's Basilica with even a teeny corner of the Campanile, the Bell Tower.

"It's perfect," said Di.

"Delightful. It really is. Let's put out our little touches of home and then go grocery shopping."

And that's exactly what they did. They had each brought some little things, things that would personalize their space and make it feel a little more like home. A small flannel lap quilt, a favourite strawberry-motifed breakfast cup, some much-loved cabbage-rose chintzy pillowcases, some teeny framed pictures of children. And off they went to the grocery store. What a ball they had, picking up all the basics. Wine and linguini and bottled tomato sauce and parmigiana reggiano and olive oil and garlic and milk and tea bags. And crusty bread and Margaret's favourite cheese, provolone picante, and a container of water buffalo mozzarella and strawberry preserves. And a teeny slice of butter and a few potatoes and onions and arugula and her passion - Italian cheese slices. They would get in the swing of it and buy the rest every couple of days from the bakeries and the markets. Oh, but they had forgotten something. While Di waited in the short line at the cash, Margaret went and picked up a bottle of Prosecco, Italy's bubbly, frothy white wine, which she absolutely adored. She also found two perfect white peaches. She was going to make them Bellinis, a drink associated with Harry's Bar and with Venice herself. Freshly-squeezed peach nectar with a generous splash of Prosecco. They were celebrating.

They walked home, arm in arm, with their baskets of goodies on their free arms, feeling very self-sufficient and, above all, ready for adventure, not to mention two of the most perfect Bellinis ever.

*****

The dance group met in a school. Margaret and Elisabetta had gone up a million steps, a million, to a large room at the top of a school. The room was a really good size and had straight-backed chairs lining all the wall and even an espresso machine in the corner. There were only a couple of people there when they first got there, but there would be more as time went on, Elisabetta said. She introduced Margaret to a few people, who all welcomed her warmly. "Piacere. Pleasure," Margaret would say. And they would answer, "The pleasure is all mine. Il piacere è tutto mio." The way people used to say, in English. A bit too formal for these days. But, in Italian, it worked. People didn't always exchange names though. Later, Elisabetta told her that there were some people who had been going for years and she still didn't know their names. Fascinating. Elisabetta also said that they rarely ever met one another outside of dancing. Also interesting. Bit by bit, more and more people did come, until, at the high point, there might have been thirty-five or forty people there. There were quite a few couples. But, interestingly enough, at one point, there were, in fact, more men there than women there. Very different from a similar event in North America.

And the guy doing the music was fantastic. He really was. He had a small keyboard, some kind of a synthesizer, and a small concertina, or accordion. No D.J. this guy. No just spinning recorded music. This guy was great. The music was exclusively Italian, with a bunch of old favourites, and some traditional pieces of music. And the dancing? Well, mostly, a lot of fox-trot, and its faster, younger brother, the quick step. And tangos, which they adored. And waltzes, some of them incredibly fast. Not everyone did those, as some of the people just weren't up for that kind of speed. There really were quite a few people there in their eighties and nineties, although one certainly couldn't tell.

Margaret had come to dance, and dance, she did. It was impolite to refuse, and besides, if one came to dance, one came to dance, no? She had noticed that she was starting to use Italian grammatical construction in English. This happened to her every time she came to Italy, and in discussions with friends who spoke other languages, Margaret had discovered that it was not at all uncommon. Bizarre, a little, but, charming, too in its own wacky way.

One little teeny guy, balding, came to get her a few times. Most of the men - most, not all - were quite a bit shorter than Margaret. One of the taller men, quite a bit taller, in fact, with beautiful gray hair and very blue eyes came to ask her to dance the mazurka. Now, by then, Margaret had danced a couple of mazurkas and she had decided that it was definitely her favourite. "Non è una valtzer. It isn't a waltz," he commented, "Si cammina. One goes for a walk." Michele, his name was, and he spoke English, quite well, in fact. He also spoke Spanish fluently as he had lived, for a while, in South America. He could really dance. What a pleasure, an absolute joy it was to dance with him. The mazurka had a part where you actually stopped for a fraction of a second...and then started up again. Like life. In some corny, cheesy way. You came to abrupt halts sometimes. But, you just had to keep moving.

At the end of the song, Michele smiled broadly at her and, with feeling, said to Margaret, "Brava. Bravissima!" "Brava" was one of those words that didn't translate perfectly. It could mean "clever" or "smart" or "great" ...but it had a connotation of "great, with heart" somehow. It was the same "Bravo!" that people said at the end of a particularly great operatic performance. It had some "Wow" in it too. And, "bravissima" was the superlative!

The teeniest guy, his name was Lorenzo, had been watching her with a real light in his eyes, in the way only Italian men can. At the end of one dance, Lorenzo said to Margaret, "Such a pity, 'peccato', that that is finished..." So sweet. Margaret danced again and again. She didn't sit down for three hours. She hadn't had so much fun in ages.

# Thank God for Red Shoes

## Chapter 3 – Energy

Before we begin, we are going to take a quick - and easy - look at quantum physics and the notion that everything is energy.

We've learned lots of wild things from quantum physics.

That one thing can be in two places at the same time - in fact, more than two!!!

That outcomes depend on observers.

We've learned those things plus tons of wild, previously unbelievable things that are expanding the very nature of science and building a bridge between science and spirituality.

For quantum physics tells us that the apparent space between the subatomic particles that make up everything - everything we experience as physical reality - is full of something.

That something is invisible, unmeasurable and all-creative. That something is powerful. That something is unfathomable.

Quantum physics also tells us that everything can exist as either a wave or as a particle. In other words, as potential or as "real". Everything can exist as an invisible potential wave in the sea of potentials or it can exist as matter, as stuff, as the things you can see.

The potential for anything and everything exists already.

This is what is called, by some, the field of potentialities.

It is the sea of possibilities - the amniotic fluid of life – and everything - every single thing - including us - is in it.

So, what is it, exactly, that turns a wave of energy, of possibility, into a particle of matter, of reality?

The answer appears to be attention and intention.

This is what Wallace Wattles, Louise Hay, Shakti Gawain, Wayne Dyer, Deepak Chopra, the people behind "What the Bleep" and "The Secret" and so many others have been saying.

Now, some people have dismissed the "manifestation formulas" – sometimes criticizing that they're too much about material accumulation and sometimes giving up, not seeing results fast enough.

As it turns out, there are very good reasons why sometimes it doesn't work instantly or doesn't appear to work at all.

The first thing is that there are lots of universal laws at work, not just one. The Law of Attraction which says that things of like energy are attracted to one another, is very powerful, but it is not the only thing at work. There are universal laws about harmony and balance, about cause and effect and many others.

Another thing that bamboozles us is that we sometimes encounter obstacles or delays. We often don't understand how we've created these.

But, trust me, every single obstacle is indeed a blessing, although it may sometimes take some time to realize it.

Every "No" from the Universe - every single "No", big or small, is telling you that it's not the right thing, not the right time, or both. Maybe something else has to be extracted.

Maybe something in you or someone else has to be refined.

There is a divine design to everything and things cannot proceed until everyone has extracted exactly what they need from a particular event, circumstance, relationship etc. We do not create in isolation. Faith is being able to appreciate this even when one feels challenged.

Lots of folks have told us this too.

The Universe is a phenomenally miraculous place - a lovely system of biofeedback. It's just amazing - truly beyond words.

The Universe is always talking to you and always listening to you - always. All catastrophe is not listening, again and again, to your own cries for balance, so much so that the message has to get louder and louder. This happens in individual lives. It also happens on the global level, as it is happening now.

If there's one thing the Universe loves, it's balance.

And, in this incredible world of energy, we are the ultimate amazing experiencers!!! We have been given the abilities to sense energies in a myriad of ways. We are the sensors. Tasting. Seeing. Touching. Healing. Feeling. Knowing. Intuiting. Reading. Laughing. Crying. Singing. Sensing. Walking. Dancing. Breathing. Learning. Experiencing. Sensing. Sensing. Sensing.

We are the oh-so privileged, truly blessed experiencers of the world.

We are the Universe experiencing itself.

Holy doodle!!!

# Capitolo Quatro

Listen to "I Hope You Dance"
by Lee Ann Womack

Padova was magnificent, a real University town, with so much to offer. Students, students everywhere. And a million bicycles. In Padova, everyone rode a bicycle. That's just the way it was. Although Padova was only a half-hour train ride away from Venice, Di and Margaret had decided to spend the night. Their hotel was just magnificent - all blue and gold - with friendly staff and one of the most amazing breakfast rooms Margaret had ever seen.

They were going to do a radio interview, Margaret's first interview of the trip. She wasn't quite sure what to expect, but how hard could it be? She had anticipated some of the questions that she might be asked on this trip and, together with Di, had formulated some potential answers. That was the only sensible thing to do. The show was live and they were going to do it in Italian. Margaret was pretty fluent in Italian, but still it was a little nerve-wracking. Still, she was as prepared as she could be, had reviewed some vocabulary that she thought she might need and so on. She had practiced the interview extensively, in English, with Di. She was as ready as she could be.

The day was beautiful, so Margaret and Di had decided to walk to the radio station, just around the corner from the Church of San Antonio. Di had gone wild over the Prato and so many things in Padova. Margaret had insisted on taking Di to see the Scrovegni Chapel and her beloved Giotto; the Anatomical Museum, part of the University; and into the Church of San Antonio. Margaret never failed to be touched by all the people who went to pray to San Antonio and who stood and touched and kissed the back of the tomb, while they prayed.

The radio host's name was Giovanni DiAngelo and he was fitting in the short interview with Margaret in the middle of his day-time radio show. It wasn't going to be very long. Giovanni was sitting in his studio when they arrived. He was very thin, with a mustache and very thick, Coke-bottle-bottom eye glasses. He motioned to her to come in.

"Allora, sei arrivata. So, you're here. Cominciamo fra poco. We'll start soon." He used the familiar form of speaking with her instead of the formal, and without asking permission, which was the custom. That seemed a little strange...

Before Margaret knew it, Giovanni was indicating that they were about to begin. In Italian, he began, "Today, we have with us Margaret Gabriel, who wrote the book, 'Thank God for Red Shoes.' What kind of psychological credentials do you have to suggest a new model of the psyche?"

Margaret was quite taken aback. So, we were going to start right in, eh? Okay...

In Italian, Margaret answered, "I did study Psychology at University, but I have no other credentials in Psychology."

"And what kind of credentials do you have in quantum physics; about which you write?"

"None," she smiled faintly.

"And, on theology, what are your credentials, your qualifications to question the traditionally-held view of God?"

"None at all. Niente affatto."

"If you have no qualifications or credentials, why should we even consider your theories other than as the ravings as a mad woman?"

Well, at least that was directly hostile…

"I am not here to convince anyone of anything. These are ideas. They are views. If you find something in them that resonates with you, that might be interesting. If you don't, that is fine too."

"So you are saying you don't care one way or another? That is quite arrogant, no?"

"I am not saying that I don't care. I am not saying that at all. I am saying that it has never been my goal to convert anyone to my way of thinking." Margaret was feeling more than a little ruffled.

"It has been suggested that this work is somehow channeled, as you say. Doesn't that make you some kind of witch really?"

"Many people who create things - be they books, or art of any kind, music, plays, sculpture, new scientific theories, choreography, discoveries of all kinds etc – will often describe the sensation as if they had their finger in the socket of the Universe. It is as if the thing is already created. Even, it seems, Michelangelo talked about this - that the figure was already in the stone - just waiting to be released. In French, we say 'ôter ce qu'il y a de trop…to take away that which is too much.' That does not make me a witch. Although, in my view, there is nothing wrong with being a witch."

"Oh, here we go. Shouldn't have said that just yet, perhaps," Margaret thought to herself.

"So you don't think there is anything wrong with being a pagan, someone who casts curses on others, an atheist, a nature worshipper?"

"There are white witches, who believe in the divine feminine and who do absolutely no harm."

"Really? Are you an atheist, then?"

"Absolutely not. Have you actually read the book?" He was starting to get to her, in spite of herself.

"But to you, God is just some aspect of quantum physics, some atoms?"

"Hardly. To me, God is everything, absolutely everything."

"Well, it has been interesting. Thank you for coming in. We have been talking with Margaret Gabriel."

Giovanni turned off the microphone.

To Margaret, he said, "An interesting discussion, Miss Gabriel," as he put back on his headphones and went back to work.

She had been dismissed.

*****

"Okay, so that was wild," Margaret lamented to Di. "I'm not sure he even read the damned book."

"Oh, I don't know. He'd read enough to question you about your credentials. At least he knew which credentials to check for," answered Di. Margaret and Di were sitting in a little bar across from the hotel. They were having a spritz, a light and delightful combination of Prosecco and Aperol, an Italian orange liqueur. "Spreetz", as the Italians pronounced it, was the favourite drink of every University student in Padova - as well as beer, that is.

"It is just going to be like that sometimes, love," Di added. "We knew this might happen to some extent. Pioneering spirit, and all that..."

"Well, okay, but now it feels pretty real. It was one thing to imagine what kind of objections or attitudes some people might bring to this content, but I guess I really hadn't expected out-and-out hostility and so personal an attack..."

"Well, get ready. Get ready to get tougher. And to keep your temper. Listen, you talk about not swallowing someone else's poison. Time to walk the talk, my dear."

"Oh, do shut up..."

"Let's have another spritz, then, shall we?" laughed Di.

Out of the blue, Margaret's Italian cell phone rang. It was Elisabetta.

"Margaret, listen. It is about Maria. Maria has had to go to the hospital. Yesterday, she was doubled over in pain and Maurizio - thank God he was there - got the doctor to come to her. Margaret, it is not good. Cancer, I think. Quite advanced, I believe. I'm sorry, but I'm not sure that she has long to live."

"Oh, no, my God, Elisabetta. Really?" Margaret started to cry. "Is that what has been going on? She really was not looking good, but I know that she is no longer a young woman... Can we go to see her?"

"Yes, I will get all the particulars and we will go as soon as you get back. When are you back?"

"Tomorrow. We're back tomorrow."

"How did it go?" inquired Elisabetta.

"I'll tell you all about it when I see you."

"Oh, oh, that sounds like a story..."

"Yes, it is a bit. Nothing to worry about though."

"Okay, teso. Ci vediamo domani. We'll see you tomorrow. I am sorry to have to tell you this way..."

"I am glad that you have. Thank you so much. Thank you for telling me..."

"Ciao, teso. Ciao. Ciao."

*****

When Margaret got back to Venice the next afternoon, she went to find Elisabetta and together they went to visit Maria. Maria looked very tiny. Very tiny indeed. She had been diagnosed with pancreatic cancer. Pancreatic. Like Patrick Swayze. Not good.

Maria smiled weakly at Margaret. "You know, there is a little boy, Niccolò, in the neighbourhood, just around the corner from the bar. A while back, I had told him that I wasn't feeling well and that he should pray for me. Well, I had forgotten about it. But, the other day, he and his Mamma were in and he came over to me. He said, 'I did it.' 'What did you do, tesoro?' I asked. And he answered, 'I prayed. I prayed for you. A lot.' The sweet cherub of a child. And Margaret, do you know how old he is?"

"No, tell me."

"Margherita, he is three…"

"How sweet…"

"Ohe, Margherita. La vita è una sofferenza… Life is but suffering…."

Maria looked very tired. They shouldn't stay too long.

"Allora, Maria….ascultami. So, Maria, listen to me. I expect to see you back at the bar very soon. Sweetness in life…that's what we all need. I want you to think about all the things that you love to do. All of them. And, when you come back, we will do them. All of them. Make me a list, okay. I'll be waiting for you; do you hear me? I am waiting for you…"

Maria smiled weakly, but she did smile.

Margaret leaned over and kissed her on her two cheeks, being careful not to hug her too hard.

Tears were welling in both Margaret's and Elisabetta's eyes as they walked down the hospital corridor. In Maria's room, a single tear rolled down her cheek. A single tear. She was cried out.

Margaret dropped off Elisabetta at her house but didn't go in, even though Elisabetta really wanted her to. As Margaret walked the long way home, her sad mind raced. How was it fair? How was it? Her melancholy stance was reflected to her everywhere. Her footsteps echoed off the stones. The Venetian stones - stones that had witnessed love and laughter, carnevale balls and burning at the stake, wondrous love affairs and countless births and rebirths, tears and death. Stones that were crumbling right now. It all felt like a giant metaphor.

Maria was so good, so sweet. What was it all about? What? Why did good people die? Was it really because they just didn't get what life was about? What else was in operation? Something... Something... It had something to do with Venice herself somehow... In some weird way...

Many people had likened Venice to an aging courtesan, but one that could go on forever nonetheless. But, make no mistake. Venice herself, grand old lady that she may be, was in great jeopardy. With rising water levels around the globe, the very existence of Venice was threatened. In Margaret's lifetime, it might be possible, even probable, that Venice might have to be abandoned completely. Beautiful, fragile, surreal Venice, who had been there forever.

But, on the scale of the life of the planet, Venice had been around for the teeniest fraction of an eye blink. It was just too tragic to contemplate. All of it. Tragic. But, a man-made city constructed entirely of islands, with foundations made of wooden poles dug into the shallow lagoon, how much of a chance did it really have with rising water levels? They were working frantically to try to find a solution, but the sad, tragic truth was there might not be an answer this time.

The Maldives were in immediate danger of disappearing forever under the water. Manhattan was in danger. Many, many coastal parts all over the planet, in fact, were in the same predicament. And so many people didn't even believe that global warming was real. She just couldn't think about it. It was just too sad. Her first lover, drowned.

Margaret would love Maria while she could. All her friends. All her family. She would love them all a lot harder. She would love Venice while she could. Love it with all her heart. Like all love affairs - like all relationships, really - with as much gusto as possible. Nothing left undone or unsaid. And, no regrets. No regrets. She would scour every each of Venezia - memorizing each contour, every nuance of her lover's face.

As she walked back through Campo Santa Maria Formosa, twilight was falling. The lanterns came on. In the distance, she could hear a gondola approaching – a tenor was singing. It was "O Sole Mio." Not Venetian at all, in fact. Rather, the song was Neapolitan, "Napolitano." It had always bugged Margaret a little how North Americans sang the lyrics incorrectly, "Oh Solo Mio". Most times they sang with an "o" at the end of "Sole" where there should be an "e." That's not how the song went at all. In truth, in the song, they were singing, in Neapolitan dialect, about their love for the sun, "il sole". "O Sole Mio!" Sole, not Solo. "Sole" is the sun; "solo" means alone. Not at all the same.

"Che bella cosa
Na giurnat'al sole
Aria serena
Dopo na tempesta"

It reminded Margaret of something else about the sun, something she had seen somewhere, on Italian television perhaps.

"Siamo tutti soli che è il plurale di sole." It was a play on words in Italian, one that didn't translate into English. "Soli" was the plural for "alone"; however, in Italian, "soli", as it turns out, is also the plural for "suns". The sentence said, "We are all alone ('soli'); but really what that word means is that we are all 'suns.'" Unfortunately, it didn't work in English - not at all. But in Italian, it was a neat play on words.

"O Sole Mio."

Not "O Solo Mio."

The gondola drifted around the corner and the song receded into the night, the last refrains echoing off the palace walls and the stones of the bridges. The sun, the symbol of life - what made it all possible.

In spite of all her grief, Margaret had one of her moments again - felt connected to it all - to everything and everyone, to Spirit, to bliss. She stopped dead in her tracks, closed her eyes, searching for her bottle. The one in which to capture the moment. And the one to capture all her tears in as well.

How on earth was she ever going to leave...?

Listen to "Do It For Love" by Hall & Oates

# Thank God for Red Shoes

## Chapter 4 - The Ego

"So what does all this have to do with ego?" you ask.

Everything.

Ego. Such an interesting word. And one that we hear a lot about these days.

Let's take a look at where the word comes from and the connotation it has taken on.

Plainly and simply, "ego" is the Latin word for "I".

Building on the work of others, Sigmund Freud used the term, ego, to describe what he saw as one of the three parts of the psyche - the ego, the id and the superego. (2)

"Id" is the Latin word for "it" and it was seen by Freud as the childlike site of the "pleasure principle" - the little kid part of us that wants what it wants and wants it right now. (3)

The superego, for Freud, was the moral component - the part that knows right from wrong but sees right and wrong as black and white with no discernment of gray. (4)

The ego was seen as the thinking, rational part of the psyche. It tried "to balance the impractical hedonism of the id and the equally impractical moralism of the superego". (5)

Freud believed that the ego, when overburdened, might employ defense mechanisms such as denial, depression and displacement. (6)

Carl Jung, another famous psychoanalyst, saw the psyche and the world a little differently from Freud and his predecessors.

Jung introduced the concept of the "shadow".

He defined the shadow as the suppressed and repressed aspects of the conscious self. He emphasized the importance of being aware of the shadow materials and incorporating them into conscious awareness, lest one project these attributes on others. (7)

Deepak Chopra, in his amazing books, "The Book of Secrets" and "Peace is the Way", talks about the shadow as the repository of negative energies. The shadow is really about fear.

Since the 1970's, the word "ego" has taken on the meaning as the thinking part of the psyche. At this point in time, we have the picture of a self-aggrandizing ego - making us identify with only our bodies, our things, our thoughts and feelings.

We have gradually come to use the term "ego" to incorporate a very broad and quite negative concept.

And, there's the rub.

Now, a lot of the time, we're actually not talking about ego at all. In truth, we're actually talking about the shadow or an interaction between the ego and the shadow together, as they certainly seem to work together.

So, here's the deal. Consider that ego's not the bad guy after all. Instead, consider that it's all just part of a system trying to stay in balance.

For it seems that the ego and the shadow seem to work together - the ying and yang, the mother and the father, the nurturer and the defender, the light and the dark, one on the love side of the equation and one on the fear side.

While the shadow is part of the defense mechanism, the part of us that deals with fear, the ego is the "I", the sense of self, the urge for recognition, for fulfillment and for the opposite of fear - for love.

This is a really big deal. A really big deal. So, how do they work? And, is it possible they actually work perfectly together?

# Capitolo Cinque

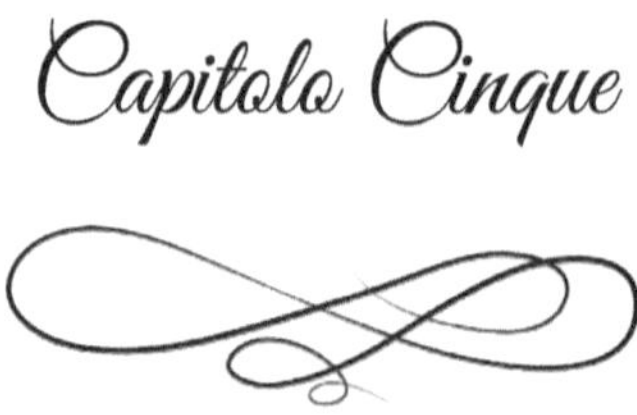

Listen to "Un Amore Cosi Grande" by Il Volo

The next few days went by in a blur. And suddenly Margaret realized that another week had passed. It was time to go to the dance circle again. She loved dancing and she loved spending time with Elisabetta. And, no doubt, she could use the distraction.

Margaret and Elisabetta wouldn't be back from dancing till 7:30 or 8:00 pm. Di hadn't felt up to it, delightful an idea as it seemed. Now that she was alone though, Di wished she had something to do after all, so she decided that she would go for a walk. In Venice, you really didn't need a destination, you could just go. She did want to go back to that little shop with all the embroidery on velvet - if she could just remember how to get there. It was on the way to the vaporetto. She had done that route a few times now, but always with Margaret. Di wasn't actually certain she could find it on her own. She headed out. The air was crisp, but there was lots of warmth in the sun, even late in the afternoon.

She made her way down the first stretch that opened up into a small piazza, and then along another little bit that looked like it went nowhere, but when you got to the end, you could see that, in fact, you could go either left or right at the end of the what-looked-like a dead end. Then along a little way, up to another bigger piazza that had a restaurant on the corner. She was just crossing a bridge, and had stopped for a second at the top of the rather steep steps to have a look at the view, when a gondolier, who was standing at the top the bridge starting speaking to her.

"Bella," the blonde gondolier said appreciatively. He was dressed in the traditional black and white horizontal stripes of the gondoliers and he was wearing his traditional hat too.

"Si, si, bella…" answered Di, gesturing at the city, a bit lamely, with her arms.

"No, non la città. Lei! No, not the city! You!"

"Me?! Ooh, you're very kind. Grazie. Thank you."

"I speak a little English. You are American?"

"No, I'm Canadian. From Canada," Di answered, somewhat stiltedly, the way one tends to do to someone who speaks another language.

"Do you like Venice?"

"Ah, yes, I love it. It's beautiful. Bellissima."

"Perhaps I can show you? Yes?"

"Oh, no, thank you. I'm meeting a friend," Di lied. Well, partially. She certainly wasn't about to go off alone with a man, a gondolier, no less.

"Perhaps another time time, then? I am Mimmo. If you change your mind, you have only to tell any "gondoliere" and they will deliver the message to me. Va bene? Okay?"

"Thank you, but I don't think I'll be going in a gondola this time…"

"Oh, please do not misunderstand. I do not mean to try to get you to take my gondola. I am trying to invite you, to show you my city, personally."

"Oh, thank you so much Mimmo. Thank you!" And, she decided that she'd better keep walking.

"Allora, arriverderci, bella. Ciao, ciao. And so, until we meet again, beautiful. Bye, bye."

Well, that was exciting. A Venetian - a Venetian gondolier, no less - had tried to pick her up! What fun was that! Although Di knew, absolutely, that Venetian gondoliers probably flirted or made the moves on every single woman they saw - eighteen or eighty. Still, it had been fun. No one had flirted with her for a long time - she remembered fondly. Vaguely!!!

*****

Margaret and Elisabetta always got to the dancing circle early. They chose chairs in their favourite corner of the room and deposited their jackets. Elisabetta went out into the corridor to get them some water. Margaret noticed, over in the opposite corner of the room, a woman who used a wheelchair and who came every week. That woman seemed to just adore dancing - she loved the music and would clap and smile the whole time. She'd keep her eyes glued on people's feet - dancing vicariously in her heart, Margaret thought. The woman's husband – at least Margaret assumed he was her husband - brought her every week. He was an amazing dancer and he took turns dancing with almost all the women there. Margaret went to talk to her.

"Don't you dance? You seem love it so," said Margaret.

"No, no..." the woman indicated the chair. She seemed to have trouble speaking.

"You know, I'm from North America. From Canada. But I speak Italian."

The woman smiled.

"There's no reason why you can't dance in the chair. Lots of people dance in wheelchairs. Shall I take you out on the dance floor?"

"No, no..." the woman looked sad. Panicked. And horrified...at the thought.

"I hope that sometime before I go home - back to Canada - I hope you'll dance."

The woman beamed at Margaret and extended her arms. She wanted to embrace Margaret. She kissed both cheeks - held onto Margaret's hands for a minute. Tears were welling in her eyes. The sweetie pie.

Elisabetta was still talking to her friends in the corridor. While they were continuing to wait for the music to begin, a woman sitting a few chairs away, said to Margaret, "If you came dancing every week, you might start to look like me." The woman chuckled. "Then again," the woman continued, "you can't expect miracles!!!" The woman snickered. Really snickered. Actually snickered. There was real meanness in it.

It dawned on Margaret that she was being ridiculed...something she knew very well from childhood. It had taken a minute for Margaret to understand that the woman was making a comment about Margaret's size. At the beginning, it had sounded conversational.

It wasn't. Not at all.

Margaret was taller than most people there and she was still heavy. Heavy. But light-footed. They had all commented on her leggerezza, how light she was on her feet. The woman, at some level, must have felt threatened somehow by Margaret - Margaret had no idea why - and had gone on the attack.

That picked at an old scar, an old scab - a "cicatrice", they said in Italian.

The music started. Thank God. A tango. There, before her, with hand extended, was a sweet man - very tall, extremely thin, ninety-one, who loved to dance with Margaret and who held her closer and tighter than anyone else, especially when they were doing the tango.

It felt stupendous to be held in someone's arms - up against someone's body. It had been...oh, my God, Margaret realized...it had been literally years - years - since she had been in someone's arms that way. It felt absolutely wonderful. Full of wonder. And, she thought to herself, astonished, she had missed it. Missed it, without even realizing it. The sheer physical pleasure of it. The sensuousness of it. Margaret felt amazing. Oh, she had hugged people and been hugged. But this prolonged embrace - this "abbraccio", the Italian word for hug - that was something else. Dancing... an extended hug. And, everyone knew, a precursor. Vertical sex, really. How fantastic!

It reminded her of something - a cute little something - that she had heard. That there was a particular denomination of religion that was vehemently against premarital sex. The punch line was that when asked, "Why is that?", the answer was not about sin, as one might expect it to be. Rather, the punch line was, "Because it might lead to dancing..." It was meant to be cute, not disrespectful, and had been told to Margaret by someone of that particular religion. Cute...

The song ended. Margaret looked in the man's eyes. She thanked him and told him that that had been wonderful. He beamed at her.

Margaret danced and danced. Tango. Fox trot. Waltz. With short and tall. With little Lorenzo. And Guido. And Paolo. Wonderful Pasquale. And beautiful Firmino. And seventeen men whose names she did not know. And with Mario, one of the best dancers there. Amazing. And amazing fun.

The mazurka started up. It had become her favourite dance. They were all her favourite, but this one was even more special for some reason. Michele - tall, charming, multilingual - appeared and extended his hand as only he could. Like a courtier. And off they went.

"You know..." said Margaret, "this reminds me of the dance in 'The Sound of Music', the dance between Maria and the Captain, on the terrace."

"I believe it is similar, if not identical," responded Michele.

At which point, Michele did something that she would remember always - something that delighted her to her toes. He changed the dance hold and led her in doing the dance - the dance on the terrace! All of it. The little kick parts as they moved first one direction and then the next. And then, to her delight – her absolutely tickled-pick delight - he did the complicated arm move so that they stood, one facing one way and one the other, with one of each of their hands linked above their heads and the other around their waists. Oh my God...it was superb. The appreciative crowd applauded as they always did when they saw someone dancing particularly well. And then, they were on their feet. Wow!!

"Oh, that was incredible..." laughed Margaret.

"It was. It was," agreed Michele. "Listen, Mario and I are going for coffee? Do you and Elisabetta want to come?"

"Let's go find out... Elisabetta, coffee, caffè?"

"I am always ready for coffee," twinkled Elisabetta, "but I have to go. I'd love to come next time though."

"It's a date..." said Michele.

*****

"What would you all like? Mario, Margaret? My treat. Offro io. Margaret, a coffee?"

"Yes, please."

"A cappuccino?"

"No, normale, grazie. No, just regular espresso, thanks."

Michele ordered everyone's drinks, picked them up from the barista and delivered their drinks to them to with a - how to express - a kind of reverence. It made an everyday thing seem really special. He brought the tazzini, the little cups, over to their table. Propped on the saucer beside the little cup, he had placed a little red-cellophane-wrapped chocolate-covered cherry. They had always been Margaret's Dad's favourites. Suddenly, she could feel him around her. Her Dad...

"Margaret…" said Mario, "you are an incredible dancer."

"She certainly is," added Michele. "You have such a strong sense of the music. You really do. It is quite amazing…almost, like you are the music."

"I am passionate about it, I am… I always have been, my whole life. I remember as a teeny child, turning on the television and dancing for hours to the music of the test pattern."

"What is a test pattern?"

"Back in the beginning days of television, the channels weren't on all day, only in the evening. It's just amazing how much has changed in my lifetime. Anyhow, during the day, they would broadcast a test pattern, it was the profile of a First Nations' person, wearing a full headdress. And, they used to play music, instrumental music. It was my first radio of my own really."

"You sound so passionate about it! What else are you passionate about? What else makes your heart sing, besides dancing?" asked Mario.

"Well…lots of things. Reading. That's one thing. Reading is simply the most wondrous thing. You voyage to other worlds, and you can create your own version of it. You are the cinematographer. You decide what the characters look and sound like. You see your version of the narrative descriptions in your mind's eye. Your own private version of the thing you are reading."

"Do you have favourites?" asked Mario.

"Oh, a million. 'The Alexandria Quartet' by Lawrence Durrell, 'My Family and Other Animals' by Lawrence's little brother, Gerald Durrell. Anything and everything by Jamie Samms, a First Nations' woman. And 'The Power of Myth' by Joseph Campbell with Bill Moyers. And historical fiction. Tons. Such a great catalyst for your imagination. When you read a book, no one else is going to have read that same book. In your mind's eye, you will have seen your very own version of the characters, imagined your version of their voices, felt your version of what they felt. It's your own version. Oh, you hear the author's voice. But it's your very own private version. So cool..."

Margaret continued, "Just recently, you know, I read a book - a couple of months ago, I guess. One of my daughters had recommended it - by David Yeadon. David's done a great deal of traveling, all over the world really, with some extended stays here and there and he's written some really fine books about his adventures. Well, anyway, in one of his books, a book of short stories really, he recounts how he and his wife, one long weekend, in New York, instead of going to the Caribbean for two or three days, stayed in their apartment and created a world of their own."

Margaret's smile deepened. "Now, I'm telling you, I could see it. I could. I could hear it. Taste it. Feel it. I was there with them. They put together a tent in the middle of their living room - complete with their mattress, lots of pillows and so on - got the finest wine and the best food to cook for each other, listened to music, made love a lot, and - listen to this - this is the best part ever - or at least I think so. It might not do anything for you. You know what he did? He read to her. Read to her. Well, that just sent me over the edge. I just about cried when I read that. 'I want one,' was my first thought. That is the most delicious, most sexy, most...I don't know... the most utterly romantic thing I've ever heard. They also generated ideas for new businesses, ate fantastic but simple meals whenever they felt like it - had the best champagne too. I love champagne."

"Listen, you are just a romantic at heart, Margherita. You have the heart of a poet..." said Michele, with great admiration.

"I wish my partner would do that for me." said Mario wistfully. "It sounds so romantic. You're right, Margherita. So sexy." Mario was gay and had been living with his partner, Sergio, for quite a long time. Mario kept trying to convince Sergio to come to the dance group, but Sergio was not having any of that. In Italy, men didn't dance together. Not yet, anyway.

"Sergio and I have been together for quite a while. We would like to be married, but that is not going to happen any time soon, not in this country."

"Why is that?" asked Margaret. "The world is changing...really rapidly. Why wouldn't it change here too?"

"We have tried and tried to get the legislation passed. But it never makes it. We thought we might be close once, when there was talk of allowing civil unions. But then, unbelievably, there was talk about any two friends being able to have such a civil union, completely missing the point and, quite frankly, being quite insulting. No, I am quite sure, it will not happen," responded Mario, with great sadness.

"Well, don't give up," answered Margaret, encouragingly. "I think that things might be changing faster than you think. Do you know that a very well-known television personality on American television, someone who had never publicly outted himself, mind you, just got married. With great support from his television show, his colleagues, and his network. Bravery, really, I want to say. But, on the other hand, and much more importantly and appropriately, how unfair is it that it should require bravery to make a statement to the world about who you love?! It's ridiculous, really. I am fortunate to live in a province and a community that is very open about such things, although it is not perfect by any means... I have many friends who are gay or lesbian, and some of them are married. Some people are mean and say, 'Why shouldn't gay people have the right to be as miserable as the rest of us?', but those are the jaded, obviously."

"Well, I wish I had your optimism."

"I am optimistic. Absolutely!!! What about you? What do you love to read?" wondered Margaret.

Mario answered, "For me, I know it is strange, but it is 'Gone with the Wind.' I have read that book a million times. It gets me every time. But, I love it... And I want Rhett Butler." They laughed. Mario looked positively awe-struck.

"For me," said Michele, "it is Dante, 'The Divine Comedy.' I know that just sounds predictable and boring. But it truly is a masterpiece, really an incredible story, incredibly told. It is 'Wow.' And, as I am sure you know, it was the beginning of the Italian language as we now think of it. Until

Dante, people all over this country spoke only their regional dialects. It was the deliberate decision of Dante to create a new vernacular, a mix of the Tuscan dialect with really practical everyday expressions from all over the place. Latin in a ballgown." Margaret loved that.

"And the story itself," continued Michele. "It is just amazing. He knew things, Dante did. He is a great technician, the way it is composed, but, most of all, he is just a fantastic story-teller. And this one, like all great literature, is full of universal truths."

"What about music?" asked Margaret. "Who do you love to listen to?"

"Ah, that is easy," said Mario. "I love anything that is profoundly sad..."

"For me," said Michele, "it is the classics. I love Caruso, and Pavarotti. I also adore Ella Fitzgerald. What about you, Margaret?"

"Well, I love the classics from the forties. And most things from the sixties. It was such an amazing time. But I love - I adore - the sucky stuff. Not the hard stuff. And I also love a lot of the stuff right now. I can't get enough of Bruno Mars...Lady Gaga. I am also crazy over Barry Manilow, and I think the Beatles were the greatest singer-songwriters ever. Right this minute, I am head over heels in love with Il Volo, the three young tenors from right here in Italy. They make me feel...spectacular."

"Music should give you goosebumps, I think," added Michele.

"Yes," agreed Mario, "or make you cry and break your heart it's so beautiful..."

"Or make you feel like you just have to dance...to move...it just makes you feel so happy," added Margaret.

"You know what the best music does?" asked Mario. "It makes you cherish - remember - or anticipate - or sometimes, forget - what it's like to be in love."

On cue, the Beatles came on the sound system in the bar, "Gotta Get You Into My Life."

"See..." said Mario, "the universe has been eavesdropping..."

62

Listen to "Gotta Get You into my Life"
by the Beatles

# Thank God for Red Shoes

## Chapter 5 - The Shadow

Let's go back to the notion of everything as energy.

Each one of us is a unique expression of energy - a unique vibration of energy. And, each one of us has been given innate detectors of energy - of the vibrations of other people, places and things.

We have been given natural devices - intuition, instinct - to detect positive and negative energies. We instinctively move toward nurturing energies and away from threatening ones. Our physiology responds automatically to perceived differences in energy or vibration. This is really what the Law of Attraction is about.

If we vibrate at similar frequencies, we are attracted - the need to feel safe and accepted is fulfilled. If we vibrate at dissimilar frequencies, we go on alert.

If the differences in vibration are slight, the sensation will be tolerable and the response relatively mild.

If the difference in our vibrations goes beyond a certain threshold, we feel alarms going off - the need to defend is indicated.

Beyond a certain threshold, certain vibrations find it hard to co-exist happily. They sense "the other." "The other" often elicits their own shadow energies. These can be likened to a predator for if not dealt with, they will potentially take your life. We are programmed biologically to instinctively, physiologically sense differences in energy.

If it vibrates the way I do, it's safe. If it vibrates differently than I do - alarm bells go off. Get ready to run or perhaps to fight!

The shadow is the place inside us that deals with "negative" energies. It deals with threats, "real" or perceived. It deals with physical threats, emotional threats, perceived threats, energetic threats - threats of all kinds. It is a defense mechanism against perceived discrepancies in energy, in vibrations.

Energies must be compatible on some level for there to be relationship.

If energies cannot be aligned, relationships may not be able to begin, to grow, or to continue. And, if relationships do have to end, trust that there is a death so that there can be a rebirth. There's always a reason for everything. Everything is about something.

In a way, the shadow is like an etheric pouch. An invisible pouch. A sieve and repository for "negative" energies. It holds memories of perceived danger, and, as well, it holds emotional toxins. Whenever you sense a discrepancy in energy, that energy is filtered through your shadow.

Yikes. As you can imagine, your shadow is a busy place. Very busy.

It's your defense mechanism. It's about fear. Fear and, of course, its many faces. Anger, frustration, grief, impatience, sadness, defensiveness, aggression and on and on.

You watch a show about something violent. In it goes. You eat something covered in pesticides. In it goes. You get into an argument with someone. In it goes. Someone makes a judgement about you when you're little. In it goes. You start believing whatever they've said. The layers start to get laid down in your shadow. These are agreements - things you've incorporated into your self-image because, when you were a little person, someone told it to you as if it were the truth!!! "You can't sing. You're stupid. You are skinny, fat, ugly, too short, too tall, too sensitive, the wrong colour, the wrong gender, blah, blah, blah, blah."

These accepted and incorporated criticisms are the plaque of your emotional being. Clogging your ability for joy.

And, on it goes.

You read a book with a description of a rape in it. In it goes. You have a job where you have to deal with a lot of people and some of them take their lives out on you. In it goes. Bless all the people who have jobs like this. Grocery store cashiers, people who work in restaurants, people who work in public service and so on.

You watch the death and devastation on the nightly news. In it goes. You hear a sorrowful sad story about abandoned little children. Or pet abuse. In it goes.

If we don't find ways to release this accumulated "negative" energy, it fills our shadow pouch to the brim. Then, "negative" energy is brimming out the top. Any little thing will prompt us to release some of it. It's got to go somewhere. And, if you cross me, even in a little way, you may just get my excess. Once the valve is opened, watch out.

Whenever you are irritated, it's because the situation has pushed your button, the one that opens the valve to your pouch of accumulated hurts, your shadow.

Especially when your reaction is disproportionate to the event, alarm bells are usually going off telling you that you've got extra steam to let off and it has nothing to do and, at the same time, everything to do with the situation that's elicited the "unwarrantedly" extreme response.

As we all know, family members are often our biggest button pushers. We let off steam with people who love us and who will forgive us and let us start again.

We see these kinds of displaced or ill-placed reactions every day, in practical ways, when something bugs us, when our shadow has sprung into action, and when we then take the "negative" energy of that and hurl it towards someone else – a third person. Trouble at work hurled towards our family. Frustration at one person directed towards a different person. Steaming mad at life, released as road rage. The adrenalin is pumping and the first person to cross us gets it.

This, of course, starts a chain reaction. Then the third party's shadow gets prompted by your "attack." Out comes hurt, anger, conflict.

"It's not me. It's you!!!" "Why are you so defensive?" "I'm not defensive. You're mean." "I'm not mean. You're overly sensitive." "I'm not overly defensive. You're grumpy." "I'm not unnecessarily offended. You're aggressive." And on and on. Point. Counterpoint. How familiar is all that?

A note that a person who's experienced a lot of abuse - who's incorporated lots of "negative" energy repeatedly - has developed a well-worn groove of response.

The sensation of pain itself has a built-in reaction - to do something that relieves the pain - something that will change the physiological sensation. Feeling good is a natural tendency. Feeling bad isn't. There is a physiological "hit" that comes from dealing with "negative" energies.

When this occurs, we have the development of a "victim" mentality. The "permanent" victim begins to interpret everything as "negative" - and sees and senses negativity even in neutral circumstances. Every time they're offended, which is often, they get a "hit". They have, in effect, become addicted to emotional pain.

And, to the extent that we are all victimized sometimes, those "negative" energies are imposed onto others, especially when their buttons are pushed. Projection.

Keep in mind that suffering is nothing but pain held onto.

All this happens on a continuum, with some of these "negative" energies being expressed when you're critical of your partner, hard on your children, known as difficult to get along with, unscrupulous, or, at the ultimate end of the continuum, evil.

On the global level, this translates as - "You hurt me." "You hurt me first." "My revenge is justified because of your injustices." "My injustices are justified because of your injustices." "My revenge is justified because of your revenge."

Where will this insanity end? A rhetorical question, but there is an answer.

When enough people on the planet understand these scenarios of war. That's when.

Especially difficult for people who are daily threatened physically by this cycle of insanity - difficult, for understandable reasons - it is up to us. Each of us.

When enough of us get it - at some magical point, we'll reach a critical mass, and everyone will get it.

You count. Big time. Someone has to be the third, the forty-fifth, the seven thousandth, the one that puts us over the top so that we all get it. Some experiments have said that number is as little as 10% of the population. Ten per cent!!

Today our shadows are in overload - anger, sadness, violence, agreements, pesticides, herbicides, toxins. Our planet is screaming at us that we are out of balance. Our bodies are screaming at us. Our weather is screaming at us. Our earth is screaming at us - earthquakes, tsunamis, hurricanes. Yes, there are some natural cycles that may explain some of this. How much? Nobody knows for sure.

No wonder these are considered the end times. We are in the process of precipitating major corrections in response to our inability or our refusal to listen to the softer messages, the more minor corrections. If we're not able to correct and correct relatively rapidly, we will experience major corrections - systems failing, natural disasters, a crisis big enough to seriously get our attention. This is just the way it works.

However, always keep in mind, that it is also the Age of Aquarius - an ushering in of a time of peace and stability, of a new beginning, of a new way of being in the world, a quantum leap, literally and figuratively, on the evolutionary path.

Above all, remember that the shadow is what allows us to experience the light. It provides contrast, the sense of duality. It allows us to experience others; it allows us to experience ourselves; it allows us to experience - period.

The physical part of the body associated with the Shadow is the liver.

There's an old story about a first-year-university Philosophy course in which the only question on the exam was "What is life?" The story went on to say that one of the Philosophy students in that class actually received a perfect mark of one hundred per cent by answering the question with a one-line answer. That answer was, "It all depends on the liver." A sentence more true there never was. It's obviously not the only organ involved - but it's a major player - a co-ordinator.

The liver performs so many functions it would make your head spin, so many that not all of them are understood. It synthesizes things, breaks down things. Many of the functions are about detoxification and purification. The liver is vital for survival and supports almost every organ in the body.

In the Zulu language, the word for liver (isibindi) is the same as the word for courage. (8)

Be kind to your liver. Be courageous.

# Capitolo Sei

Listen to "Un Angleo Disteso al Sole"
by Eros Rammazzotti

The train to Rome was amazing. New. Fast. Comfortable. Beautiful. They came around with espresso - of course, they did. Both Di and Margaret were excited about the trip to Rome. Some time to see the City. Margaret had been there before, but just for teeny visits, usually on the way to somewhere else, but not Di. Where to begin, that was the question. The big things, the obvious things – the Colosseum, the Forum, the Spanish Steps, the Trevi Fountain, Piazza Navona, the Palatine Museum, the Pantheon...oh, where to start? What should one do the first time in Rome? And the Vatican! St. Peter's and the Sistine Chapel. And on and on. One could spend a lifetime and still not see it all. And those were just some the obvious things.

They had decided to stay in Trastevere, on the other side of the Tiber River. Trastevere was charming, it just was. The hotel they were staying in was very near the Campo dei Fiori, and across the river from the Jewish ghetto. It was small and intimate, nestled in a charming little neighbourhood with other small hotels and lovely little restaurants. Outside the train station, Di and Margaret had hopped in a taxi and asked the driver to take them to Piazza Trilussa. He was sweet and talked to them about a cousin in Calgary and how he wished he could get to Canada sometime as he had heard it was very, very beautiful. He asked if they were sure that they didn't want him to take them closer to the hotel, but Margaret assured him that they were happy to walk the rest of the way.

They put their luggage in their rooms and marvelled at the city, right at their feet, just outside their windows.

"Listen, I need to phone Rosie," said Di. Rosie had been a friend of Di's since they had been in high school together in Coburg. Rosie had come to Rome a dozen or so years ago and fallen in love with a dashing Roman. She'd never come home.

"I'm so looking forward to seeing her. We're going to confirm our dinner date for tomorrow. I haven't seen her for so long and we have a ton to catch up on. Are you sure you won't join us?"

"I'm sure, I'm sure. You and I are going to have a nice dinner together tonight at my favourite little spot around the corner - so good - and tomorrow, the two of you need some time alone to catch up. Besides, after that interview tomorrow, the last thing I'll probably feel like is going out. I'm still quite anxious about it. It's one of the really big things we have to do this trip."

"You have absolutely nothing to worry about. You are a natural. And Ricky, this guy who's interviewing you, seems to be really good. Really professional. And a perceptive interviewer."

"Well, after Padova, I still feel a little trepidation. Just a little..."

"You'll be fine. I know you will. Now, let's get your mind off it. Where are you going to take me first?"

"Well, I know how interested you are in Kabala...so, I think we should start with the Ghetto, just back across the river. And maybe up to the Palatine Museum. We'll see..."

"And then, tonight?"

"Tonight, we are going to have Fettucine Alfredo and then go for another nice long walk, maybe to the Trevi Fountain, and we'll stop for gelato. Sound okay?"

"Sounds heavenly. Heavenly."

*****

Ricky Delvecchio was gorgeous. A huge man. Probably six three, at least. Heavy, but he could handle it. A beautiful face, just beautiful. But it was his personality that was the killer. He had charisma. To spare. Everybody loved Ricky. He was a household word in Italy, truly beloved. A "simpaticone", they said. And a real character. Witty and warm. Spirited. A gourmand. A ladies' man. In love with life. It showed. Ricky glowed. He just did. He had, over the years, developed quite the career in the Italian television industry. He had hosted only the most popular shows for a good many years. He was bigger than life. A huge personality. And, a really lovely man.

He was the host of "Intervista", a series of interviews with international stars, a show that was incredibly popular in Italy these days. Top-rating kind of stuff. Margaret was lucky to be invited onto such a show. Ricky had interviewed George Clooney, and Sophia Loren, and Tony Blair, and Jude Law and many others…big names.

Ricky's staff was very professional. A car had been sent for her to collect her from her hotel. They would conduct the interview in English and they would dub in the Italian. The producers had talked to her in depth about her book, but said that Ricky never gave a list of his questions ahead of time to the people who were about to be interviewed. He just didn't. It messed up his spontaneity, he said. The show was taped in front of a live audience.

Margaret was ready. Ricky also didn't like to meet or greet the guests ahead of time. He wanted it all to be quite authentic. Margaret and Di had been treated like VIPs. Ricky's beautiful Executive Assistant, who was also named Diana, had shown them into the Green Room and settled them, making sure they were comfortable. She was stunning, with long, chestnut hair and a spectacular face and she was dressed impeccably in a white suit and four-inch stilettos - red. The three women had enjoyed that two of them had the same name, Diana, although it was pronounced quite differently. And the Italian Diana had laughed, delighted with the shortened form of "Di". It sounded just like "Dai" in Italian, which you could hear virtually everywhere and which meant, "Come on…"

Margaret and Di had been offered cappuccini or caffè latte; Prosecco; cornetti, those delicious Italian croissants; a stupendous fruit platter. As the time approached for the filming to begin, Margaret was ushered into the guest seat on the set, a beautifully comfortable deep blue velvet chair, by Diana, who had been beyond kind, beyond welcoming. "He'll be along shortly. Are you comfortable? Can I get you anything? Ricky always has a coffee just before he starts. Would you like to join him?"

"Yes, thank you, that would be really nice."

And then, there he was, even more impressive in real life than he was on television. Margaret had watched some of Ricky's previous shows on video. They didn't do him justice. There was one thing, though, that confused her. He was self-deprecating about his weight. Completely unnecessary, in her opinion. At one point, on one of the shows, Ricky had made more than one derogatory remark about his own weight, saying them as though they were funny. How strange. That he should refer to himself that way. What was all the self-deprecation about? It obviously was a soft, sore point for him. Interesting… Ricky, nonetheless, or perhaps partially because of it, was one of the most personable people she had ever seen, let alone met. It made him vulnerable. Human. Accessible. And, to boot, Ricky was very, very handsome. Beautiful, even.

The crowd went wild.

"Benvenuti tutti. Benvenuti. Welcome everyone. Welcome." His voice was incredibly deep, an exclamation mark at the end of every sentence. "Tonight we are in for a real treat. We have with us, Margaret Gabriel, author of 'Thank God for Red Shoes', that insightful book that is getting us to think about things with new eyes. And tonight, right after this first commercial pause, she is all ours. Tonight, Margaret Gabriel on 'Intervista!'" Ricky announced, with purely Italian flourish.

Just as the commercial was coming to an end, Ricky came over to Margaret and gave her a wink. He downed his coffee. "What a charmer," she thought to herself. As they started up again, Ricky opened his arms and kissed her cheeks, each a little longer than necessary.

"Welcome, Margaret, a bellissima Margaret, I might add. May I call you Margaret?"

"Yes, of course…"

"We are very happy to have you with us tonight. It is a real pleasure. I have read your book, actually, a few times. Your book is very readable and has many interesting ideas. Every time I read I find something new in it."

"I am delighted to be here…"

"Margaret, please tell us about the basic premise of your book."

"Well, it is basically that we have misunderstood the function of the 'ego' and that rather than it being an unpleasant kind of character, the way we talk about it making us identify with superficial things, that it is actually a supremely positive function of the psyche."

"And can you tell us briefly how that is so?"

"I'm not sure I can do it briefly but it is basically this. That our psyche actually is constructed with two sides, if you will, that need to be in balance. One side is about love, about nurturing, about the light, about the 'feminine' in some ways and the other side is about fear, which I believe is the opposite of love, about defense, about the dark, about the 'masculine' in some ways. One side helps us to keep things with 'positive' energy circulating through us and one sides helps to protect us from things with 'negative' energy. We need both. We want nurturing and protection," Margaret smiled.

"And," she continued, "like all things in nature, we need to be in balance. The 'ego', I believe, is not on the negative side at all, but rather on the positive side, with its alter-ego, if you will, the 'shadow', opposite it. I see them both as etheric, energetic pouches, one for positive energies and one for negative energies. Our job is to keep the negative energies that we absorb over the day and over our lifetimes circulating out of the negative pouch, the 'shadow,' and to keep the positive energies we need to be in balance circulating into the positive pouch, which I believe to be the 'ego.'"

"And the 'shadow' is a concept of Carl Jung's?"

"Yes, that's right."

"Why do you think that the concept of 'ego' has taken on such negative connotations, unless they were warranted?"

"Well, that is a complicated question and I don't know the answer for certain. But, because the 'ego' - in the book, at least - provides a function of urging us towards pleasurable feelings, I think that the 'ego' became associated with the idea that to feel good is to be bad, somehow. I don't believe that. I believe, in fact, that we are here to feel good, to experience as much happiness, joy and contentment as we can."

"Isn't that a pretty superficial way to live? Pretty narcissistic, in fact?"

"It would be superficial if it meant being happy about superficial things - temporary, fleeting ways of feeling good. But I am talking about much more fundamental, more basic things. Things like loving your family and friends; and being of service to your neighbours, to your community, to the community of the planet; and relishing the beauty of the amazing world we live in; and the joy of music and dance; and the sensation of no-time that comes from creativity; the power of gratitude and of forgiveness; and the indescribable feeling of fulfillment, of living a life on purpose. That sort of thing."

"Margaret, are you a Christian?" asked Ricky, looking straight through her.

"Okay, so here we go..." she thought.

"I believe in the essential truths, in what's at the the core of all religions. I believe in compassion, in kindness, in love, in forgiveness, in empathy, in miracles, and, most of all, in God. I believe in the truths of Jesus, yes, certainly, as do I believe in those of Jehovah, Mohammed, Buddha, Shiva,

Lao Tse, the Great Mystery of many aboriginal and First Nations peoples, the Goddess and many other spiritual beliefs. I don't think that God sits in judgement, nor do I think that God is observing us to see if we sin so that we can be forgiven."

"Do you not believe in sin then?"

"I do not believe in sin, per se, as we currently understand it. I believe that we all have, within us, the potential for good and for evil. Of course, I believe that there are things that are right and things that are wrong. But I also believe that the traditional concept of sin had a lot to do with misogyny. Women were bad. Temptresses. Wicked. Women were to blame for the bad in the world. Women and therefore sex were bad. Sinning had a lot to do with the assumed wickedness of women. Unfortunately, ... Such nonsense, in my opinion."

"Have you never sinned, then?"

"Have I ever done something wrong, something that I knew in my heart was wrong? Yes, of course, I have. But I do not think of that as sin, in its traditional definition."

"And do you feel no remorse?"

"Yes, of course, I feel remorse, and I try to learn from situations so that I don't repeat mistakes."

"Would you not feel better knowing that you were forgiven?"

"Yes, of course, but I believe we are all already forgiven. That we live in a constant state of grace. And that I, and perhaps we all, have to work, hardest of all, to forgive ourselves."

"How, Margaret, would you describe what is 'sacred'?"

"I think that many things are sacred - life itself, breath, being of service, love, creativity, open-mindedness, gratitude, laughter also."

"You don't think that solemnity is important?"

"I think that there are some times that solemnity is sacred, when it is heart-felt, for instance, I also think that laughter can be sacred, in fact, very sacred indeed."

"Have you been to Church here, in Italy?"

"Yes, many times."

"Isn't that hypocritical of you?"

"Not at all. There is great sacred energy and spiritual power in the gathering of people together to worship God. Of any religion. People expressing their love of God, their gratitude to God, people raising their voices in unison, people in prayer, people singing. These are all very powerful things."

"You say you love Italy. Don't you think that it is insulting to come here and criticize the basic fundamental beliefs of the entire nation?"

"I am not criticizing the beliefs of anyone. I am suggesting a theory about energy - a model."

"But you do think the Church has lost its relevance, don't you?"

"That is such a difficult question. I think that, fundamentally, people want something to believe in. They just do. But that thing they believe in has to have relevance for their everyday lives. There is absolutely no doubt that traditional religions offer that for many, many people and will continue to do so, as they have in the past. For some, however, a new perspective is welcome. And, in fact, may actually lead some people back to God."

"What would you say to Muslims, for instance, who say that there is only one God and that that is their God?"

"I think one has to be supremely respectful and sensitive about people's beliefs. I share the belief that there is one God and I believe that that one God is the same God to everyone. That is my personal belief. The dogma is different from religion to religion. But, to my view, God is God, regardless of the name used. I believe that God is the Source, the universal intelligence and consciousness, the Creator. I am not, in any way, commenting on or criticizing anyone else's beliefs. I believe that in every religion and spiritual belief on the planet that there have been people - some say 'angels', some say 'prophets', some say 'shamans', there are many other words, I am sure - very connected to Spirit, who have come to know many fundamental things - universal truths. Each one of those connected people, or societies, interpreted what they heard, what they saw, what they knew, in the language and in the imagery - in the context, really - of their time and their culture - and, often, using metaphor. Not only that, but across the years, and with much translation, some of the original concepts may have been altered, or possibly lost."

"As Joseph Campbell pondered, why do we interpret the poetry of our beliefs and stories and enduring myths of the world, as if they were prose? As if every word was literal?" said Ricky, thoughtfully.

"Exactly," smiled Margaret. "Appunto."

"So, how do you think the Catholic Church feels about your theories?"

"I have no idea. The theories are not meant to refute or threaten anyone or anything."

"Margaret, in your book, you also have some very interesting ideas about illness and about addictions. Can you tell us about those? What about illness?"

"Well, it seems that when a person's system is out of balance and starts to accumulate too much negative energy and if that energy has no release, one starts to experience some kind of discomfort or dis-ease. Illness seems to be a biofeedback way of letting a person know that they are out of balance. Negative energies that haven't been able to be dissipated somehow seem to have to be expressed as something and that something seems to be illness, either physical or, sometimes, mental. Those negative energies themselves can be either physical, like pollution, or emotional, like resentment, for example."

"And addictions?"

"Addictions, on the other hand, seem to develop in response to a great need to feel better. If a person is living in balance, they don't need so many temporary fixes of good feeling. But if they are out of balance, they need to do something, anything to feel better. Those things can include drinking, smoking, eating, gambling, shopping etc. If the imbalance continues though, and the person continues to use these superficial ways of feeling better, they often find that they need more and more of the comforting behaviour, as over time, it seems to diminish in its ability to comfort. The birth of addiction..."

"And, Margaret, what about evil? Do you believe in the devil?"

"I believe that evil can be the ultimate imbalance of negative and positive energies, but I also believe that we are all born with the capacity for ultimate good, or ultimate bad, depending on our circumstances."

"And the devil?"

"I'm not sure about the devil. Although I do think that the ultimate good, God, and its opposite, the ultimate bad, can both have voices, if you will."

"Margaret, Margaret, we have, so truly unfortunately, used up all our time. Such a very great pity. But I thank you so much for agreeing to talk with us, and there is still so much to discuss. I could have asked a million more follow-up questions about every single topic we touched on. I certainly invite you to join us again, when you can, to continue and to delve deeper into our very interesting discussion. Everybody, please give Margaret a warm round of applause. Good night everybody and che Dio ci benedica... may God bless us."

*****

"Oh, Margaret, that was fantastic!!! Just fantastic!!" Ricky was very energized. After the taping, he always spent a lot of time greeting the people in the audience and, this time, he invited Margaret to join him in shaking the hands of anyone and everyone who wanted to do so. Di was still off with Diana.

"Thanks, Ricky, I really enjoyed it too."

"Wasn't too tough on you, was I? I figured you could handle it. And you did. Quite magnificently in fact."

"Thanks. You are a great interviewer. You made it easy."

"Have you been to Rome before, Margaret?"

"Yes, a few times."

"Do you know the city well, then?"

"No, not really. Somehow, I also seem to be on my way to somewhere else, when I come through Rome..."

"That's such a pity, Margaret. It really is beautiful, not just superficially, but, its heart, its soul, you know. That is even more beautiful. Listen, are you busy this evening? I would love to show you my city, through my eyes though, not through the eyes of a visitor? Or how about dinner? Could I take you to dinner?"

"Oh, Ricky, that would be so nice of you. Are you sure it's not an imposition?" She just could not refuse. She couldn't.

"No, beautiful lady, the pleasure is all mine. I know just the place. Shall I pick you up from your hotel?"

"Oh, yes, please, if you don't mind. Usually, I would say that I would meet you at the restaurant, but the city is immense and I don't know it very well at all."

"I wouldn't hear of it. Where are you? And are you with someone? Ah, your publicist? Someone else? We could include them, of course."

"I came to Rome with Di, my friend and also my publicist, but she is busy tonight."

"That is the answer I was hoping for, I must admit. Where are you staying?"

"I am in Trastevere, at the Albergo Santa Maria. Do you know it?"

"Yes, yes, I know it. And it is only steps from where we will go to dinner. I shall come to collect you, say 8:00 o'clock. Is that good for you?

"Yes, that's fine. I'll see you then."

He kissed her hand then, "I am so looking forward to it, my new friend. Until tonight then. Arrivederci." And then he kissed both her cheeks.

"Oh, my..." she thought. What had she gotten herself into?

Listen to "Bewitched, Bothered and Bewildered"
by Rod Stewart & Cher

# Thank God for Red Shoes

## Chapter 6 - The New Old Ego

And so, back to the ego - at least, our new understanding of it.

Just as your shadow is the repository for "negative" energies, its counterpart, your ego, is the repository for "positive" energies. It is the home of what feels good - that inimitable urge for bliss - the urge for fulfillment, the urge for creativity, for peace, for satisfaction, for love from others evolving into self-love and the love expressed to others, for acceptance, for recognition, ultimately for our Godliness.

This urge is strong. Inexorably strong. Our sense of self wants to be expressed. Ultimately, there is an urge to recognize that we are Spirit - all of us - each one of us. There is also a simultaneous urge to recognize that the personalities and bodies that we wear, although not the true us, are temporary but priceless gifts to be enjoyed to the fullest. We're meant to recognize both that we're God made manifest and that our physical manifestation is the greatest - the very greatest of presents. Presence.

The ability to experience coupled with the knowledge that we are intrinsically part of the creative source of everything!!!!

Now, that's a big deal. A really big deal.

Don't let anyone tell you otherwise.

Ego is the desire for love. It's the part of you that wants to be loved, to feel good, to be touched, to be seen, to be listened to, to be recognized, to be validated, recognized as what you truly are - a divine being. It starts out wanting all that from someone else - a loving, protective, nurturing, defending parent - so it can learn to get that ultimately from itself and then to give it to others.

This is the part of you that wants to be admired. It wants to be accepted, admired and respected by others, but ultimately it wants to be validated by itself - or rather, by personality, with whom it is personally and inexorably linked.

It's a desire, given to you by Spirit, to motivate your personality to use the gifts you've been given in the service to humanity. Your passions are God's way of letting you know what service you are to provide to humanity, to creativity and to evolution.

Follow your bliss, be the best you that you can be, doing what you love and doing it as only you can do it, your calling. And do it, loving every aspect of yourself. Embrace yourself, flaws and all.

And so it follows that ego is the etheric pouch for positive energies - a counterpoint to, and foil for, the shadow.

Someone cares for you. In it goes. Someone says something good about you. In it goes. You have a talent and you share it. In it goes. You have a warm, wonderful conversation. In it goes. You get positive attention. In it goes. You have a serendipitous connection, a connection that makes you feel so happy, with a stranger. In it goes. You have moments of connection to Spirit. In it goes.

If you're living your life to the fullest extent; if you're using the talents and skills, you have; if you're helping others; if you're developing your potential for something; if you're experiencing the positive aspects of learning; if you're feeling the joy of all that - you will have a very happy ego - a satisfied ego.

A satisfied ego helps to keep the shadow at bay.

Your job is to keep good things circulating into the good pouch and to keep circulating bad things out of the bad pouch.

Left, right, left, right... It is a moment for people on the planet to honour their own red shoes. The right and the left, both. Occasionally, step ball change. A dance move.

In many indigenous cultures, unique skill sets and talents are held in high esteem. For example, in "Mutant Message Down Under", by Marlo Morgan, a story about a woman who gets to experience the Outback with aboriginal people, each individual is respected and, in fact, named for the unique things at which they excel, their particular talents. Their particular gifts. Each individual is honoured...truly honoured. And they fall naturally into their position as they work together towards the good of all. (9)

Every one of the indigenous people automatically finds her or his niche and does what she or he is good at. They understand that each person comes with her or his own talents, propensities and gifts. It is the most natural thing in the world to do what you are naturally good at and which appeals to you. It is spoken of with pride by the others - "She is the one who... He is the one who..."

Here in North America, so often we try to make everybody the same and to foster competition. We send children to school, reward those who have natural academic talents and can learn in a visual, staying-still way but often we are challenged by those whose talents are not recognized as "valuable" or those who learn differently. We assess people's natural academic talents, praise those that have them and often marginalize those that don't seem to display them in a conventional way. According to our somewhat skewed standards of what people should know and how they should learn.

We need a revolution in our education system.

If only we could, more and more, find ways to recognize and encourage the potential for the unique expression of each soul. Some schools and some teachers are doing this now. Let's applaud them. Encourage them. Promote them. Model their way of educating.

There are incredible individuals who do this now and we need to recognize them. We need to do it at the systemic level. With a broader brush. Teaching self-esteem. The one big thing we all seem to lack.

We need to get uniformly and systemically better at this.

We need curriculum reform; careful consideration of class size and configuration; revitalized teacher training; and a philosophy that provides truly excellent basic skills coupled with an encouragement to approach learning and life with passion and creativity. Better English, better Math and Science, the Arts, Vocational skills, alternative forms of assessment for alternative learners, practical skills, life skills and an appreciation for empathy and for other cultures. New definitions of success, in both the academic sense and in life. Opportunities for real learning instead of busy work. Don't get me started!

Just a generation or so ago, as little kids in elementary school, we had a text book that was called "Anchors and Sails." Where the heck are they - those anchors and sails?

Each child needs to be encouraged each day.

Implicit underneath this is the requirement of a shift in our world view.

We currently maintain a deterministic view of the world, one where we associate "success" primarily with money and with the accumulation of things. Furthermore, so often, we do this not by doing what we love, but by doing the practical thing, the thing we should "fall back on" and by this alone. As long as we continue to do this, we will continue to live part of our lives in a hollow shell. So many of us have accumulated so much stuff, that now it's just a pain, nothing but clutter. So many of us have forgotten our dreams that we live a life unlived.

Of course, we need a certain amount of money for the necessities and the pleasures of life. However, look at "The Spirit Level" by Kate Pickett and Richard G. Wilkinson. You will see a convincing argument that you can improve the psycho-social well-being of the majority of a population, not by raising standard levels so much as by reducing income differences between the rich and the poor. (10)

In other words, we all need a certain amount of money but, beyond that amount, how much money there is in your bank account is not necessarily indicative of how happy you are. It just isn't. It isn't how rich you are, how beautiful you are, how talented you are, how popular you are. It just isn't. Ask Lindsay Lohan, Charlie Sheen, and so many others.

Our current world crises are urging us to return to valuing what is important - listening to your calling; relationships with loved ones - family, friends and community; the joy of simple things; trustworthy neighbours; kindness; old-fashioned fun; helping others; gratitude; forgiveness; happy experiences and memories; compassion and love and real meaning to your life.

If only we would allow and encourage our children to identify and live their passions. To express their natural talents. They are given abilities, propensities and interests, as are we all, as clues as to what contribution they and we are to make to humanity in this lifetime. Let's find ways to foster this.

Some teachers and many homeschoolers do this successfully now - exposing their children to a rich environment of topics and letting the learning become student-directed. This produces children who love to learn. They are self-motivated, self-directed learners.

It is possible to live our passions.

The conviction with which we present this to our children, of course, depends upon our own deeply-felt belief that it is true. We have to truly believe that you can do what you love to do and still have a "good" life, so often, erroneously translated as only money. Don't get me wrong - there's nothing intrinsically wrong with money. It, however, pales in comparison with personal fulfillment.

Interestingly, the ego is affiliated with the hands and feet.

When we are infants, and if we are fortunate, our parents or caretakers, fulfill our needs.

We are held, fed, kept warm, rocked, changed and loved, all by loving hands. As we grow older, loving hands hold ours. We start to clap in delight. Clap in absolute delight. Some of our needs start to be met by our own hands. From others, the patting, soothing and comforting all nourish our sense of wellbeing. Our crawling makes us mobile. Exciting.

And, then, we stand. On our own two feet. Hands and feet. Hands and feet.

Applause. Congratulations. Standing. Holding hands. Walking. Taking a stand. Standing on your own two feet. Standing up for what you believe in. Handshakes. Hugs. Hands, sometimes used against you. Waggled fingers. Healing hands. Clapping rhythmically. Dancing. Making music. Creating. Art. Making tools. Making love. Preparing food. Wow. Hands and feet are something else.

We want happy hands from others. Expressions of praise. The pat on the back. The hand extended in greeting. We want to feel fulfilled. We want to feel loved. Without it, we languish.

This carries on in sometimes more symbolic terms. We want to feel accomplished. We want to feel recognized. We want to feel appreciated.

Want to help satisfy your ego, your urge for fulfillment?

Use your hands and use your feet in loving ways.

Make something. Love someone. Hug somebody. Extend a hand in friendship. Pat a pet. Cook something. Draw something. Use your hands in some loving way. Write something. Paint something. Walk in nature. Stand on your own two feet. Walk into someone else's life and offer helping hands.

And, what else helps your ego?

Facing fear, that's what.

The more you face your fears, the more empowered you become. Show your shadow that it is not going to immobilize you and your happy ego will soar with empowerment. What gives you the most satisfaction is the sense of dealing effectively and successfully with your shadow. Learn to live in the outer boundaries of your comfort zone. Learn the art of discernment of fear that is in response to something truly threatening to your life as opposed to fear of something that stretches you.

Let your shadow overpower you and you'll have an ego that's got nowhere to go but down.

"Down to where?" you ask.

Our model needs to expand to answer that question.

# Capitolo Sette

Listen to "Locked Out of Heaven"
by Bruno Mars

Promptly at 8:00 pm, there was a call from the desk, "Signora Gabriel, il Signore Delvecchio is here for you."

"I'll be right down. Thank you. Arrivo subito. Grazie." Margaret had to admit she had taken extra care with how she looked. She wore red and she looked gorgeous. She really did. And, she felt great. It showed.

"There you are. Ah, Margherita, you take my breath away..." Ricky had, with a very natural ease, used the Italian version of her name, "Margherita", a word that also meant "Daisy". She was "Margaret" no more.

"Well, thank you, Ricky. You look very beautiful yourself," she answered.

He laughed, a hearty, real laugh, all the way to his eyes. He did look spectacular, in a dark suit; a perfectly-starched, pristine white shirt; and a beautiful dark pink - yes, pink - tie. He was right off a magazine page. Her hormones went into overdrive, in spite of themselves. Oh, my God, she was in trouble.

He took her hand and led her through the revolving door. Once outside, Rome assaulted them - deliciously. Very naturally, he put his hand in the small of her back as they walked together. An intimate act, no doubt.

"Trastevere is a wonder, isn't it?" Ricky asked, not really expecting an answer. "Have you been to see the Raphaels just around the corner?" There were the most incredible paintings of Raphael's right there, steps from her hotel.

"I have, you know, more than once. I never fail to marvel."

"Do you enjoy Italy's art then?"

"That is an understatement. You know, the first year I ever came here, I bought a paperback copy of Vasari's 'Lives of the Artists.'"

It was a book that every serious Italian Art History student knew, a book of biographies of artists, especially of the 1400's, written by a contemporary of theirs and, of course, an artist in his own right, Giorgio Vasari.

"I have carried that book around for so long now, that it is dog-eared beyond belief. The spine is cracked - pages are loose," added Margaret.

"A sign that it has been well-loved, I am sure. I know you speak Italian; I have heard you. Italian literature, do you know it, too?"

"Where did you hear me speaking Italian?" She couldn't imagine.

"On the radio," answered Ricky.

"Oh, dear, that wasn't the best interview, was it?" Ricky smiled and shrugged. That Italian who-gives-a-damn - 'chi-se-ne-frega' face, so perfect...

"È uno stronzo, quello. He's a shithead, that one," Ricky commented, not impressed with Giovanni in Padova.

Margaret laughed. "To answer your question, yes, I've read 'Promessi Sposi', and 'Il Gattopardo' and 'Cristo si è Fermato a Eboli'..."

"In Italian?!"

"Yes, in Italian. With a dictionary beside me, naturally...but yes, in Italian."

"Ah, I am very impressed. Very. And anything else?"

"I am about half way through Dante's 'Divine Comedy', but, I must confess that I am reading that in English…"

"Ah, yes. In Italian, it is very difficult. Very… Even for us… And where did you learn to speak Italian so 'divinamente' - so divinely?"

"In Venice. A million years ago, on a Summer School course. It was a turning point in my life. We learned so much, so fast. And I had an astounding professor, who has since become my beloved friend. He also is an exquisite poet. I should let you read some of his poetry some time. It is staggeringly beautiful."

"I would love that. A friend, eh? Or perhaps, a lover?" Ricky suggested, cocking his head.

"No, no, not that. But a very dear friend. I love him like the big brother I never had. And he was a professor like no other. Challenging, charming, difficult, wonderful, sometimes torturing. But one of the best professors I ever had, and I had some good ones. And, he is still one of my best friends, after all these years."

It felt magnificent to walk beside him, with him. Margaret caught a glimpse of herself and Ricky, the two of them, in the display window of a clothing store they were passing. They looked amazing together. People were recognizing Ricky but he wore it easily. Together, they attracted even more attention, although Margaret didn't recognize it as that.

"Ah, look," he said, "we are already here." With immense warmth, Ricky greeted the Maitre D. "Ciao, ciao, Roberto. Guarda, ti voglio presentare una mia grande amica, la Canadese famosa, Margaret Gabriel. Hi, hi, Roberto. Look, I want you to meet a great friend of mine, the famous Canadian, Margaret Gabriel."

In impeccable English, Roberto responded, "Ah, good evening Miss Gabriel. I am Roberto and I am a great fan of yours. I hear that you will be on Ricky's show. We are delighted to see you. Please, come in. We have a special table for you."

The restaurant was everything she'd expected and more. Stone walls, all in candlelight, impeccable white tablecloths, the loveliest staff. And many Romans - all beautiful, dressed to the nines, with a very uniquely Roman sophistication, a certain something that set them apart somehow. Ricky sat right beside her, rather than across from her. They were very close.

"I thought that we would start with Prosecco. Would you like that, or would you prefer something else?" asked Ricky, ever-attentive.

"Oh, I would like Prosecco. I just love it, you know."

"Here's to you, my bellissima Margherita. Salute. To your health."

"And to you... Salute. Cin cin."

The wine was dry and cold and delicious. Ricky leaned across the table and kissed her gently on the mouth, lingering a moment.

"Forgive me," he smiled mischievously, not looking at all like he wanted forgiveness whatsoever. "I've been wanting to do that from the first moment I laid eyes on you. Now, would you like to see a menu, or shall we ask Roberto what he would suggest?"

"Oh, definitely, Roberto's recommendation," Margaret answered. She was feeling a little breathless.

Dinner was magnificent. Their conversation was easy. They had a lot in common. And Ricky was used to a life where he made conversation for a living. But, it wasn't just that. He had great stories to tell and really knew how to spin them. He was also just a magnificent listener, and made her feel like everything she talked about was the most fascinating thing he had ever heard.

They started with a lovely antipasto of traditional bruschetta, with new olive oil and salt, served with caramelized onion marmalade. Delicious.

"Buon appetito, tesoro," he said. "Eat well, darling."

"Altretanto. Same to you," Margaret answered in Italian. They actually had been speaking in both English and Italian and going back and forth. It was a heady experience. She loved it. There was something about using a language other than one's mother tongue that was intoxicating. And, going back and forth, between two languages, well, that seemed to produce even more endorphins, for some reason. She felt deliciously light-headed.

The 'primo', the first course, was tagliatelle, hand-made egg noodles, delicate and delicious, with mixed wild mushrooms. The 'secondo', the second course, was roast chicken, perfectly cooked and delicately seasoned, accompanied by a plate of sautéed kale, so delightful, and the best fried potatoes she had ever had, and, finally, a light green salad, with 'puntarelle', chicory shoots and a touch of oil and vinegar. They drank red wine, dry, smooth, like velvet on her tongue.

"I've noticed that in photos of you, you are often are wearing this bracelet and it looks like it says, 'Eleven, eleven'? Are you interested in numerology? What is its significance?"

"Yes, I am, although I haven't studied that much about it. Eleven, eleven, 1111, is about new beginnings. But, you are interested in numbers too, aren't you? I heard you, on one of your television shows, say that the number 7 was very important to you. I think you said it was your birthday."

"Yes, that's right. What an interesting thing for you to remember..."

"Yes, I'm not sure why that stuck. But it did. Which month?"

"August..."

"Ah, that makes you a Leo. That makes sense, actually, from what I have seen on your television shows. I think you are a very stereotypical Leo, are you not?"

"'Ebbè', ah, Margherita, well, yes, it is true. I think you could say that. The good of it and the bad… What do you think about astrology? I gather that you think it has validity?"

"Oh, sure, I do. But, that's because of one of these theories, you know, the kind that just seem to come to me…"

"I am interested in this theory. What is it?"

"Allora, well, you see, it's come to me that it was not the light that was created, but, rather, the dark. That, instead, light always existed, always was, always. Always will exist… But it was all together, with nothing else. Nothing but light. And that the "big bang", well, that "big bang", whatever it was…well, it actually created the dark. That and, as well, simultaneously, it dispersed all the light into bits of light, if you will. That was the 'let there be light' part."

"In other words, the Source - God or whatever name or concept you want to use - well, that that pure love, and the creative source of everything, always was, always existed, always. However, at some point, some kind of deliberate intention seems to have created the universe, as we think we understand it anyway. Suddenly, we have duality, and with that duality, with that contrast, we have the birth - well not really the birth, the birth was its conception as an intention, but you know what I mean - the birth - the beginning - of experience itself."

"Wow…"

"I know… The potential for sensation becoming sensation itself. So stunning, really, to think about… And the light, that God-light, was dispersed as discreet entities, well seemingly so, because, it fact it was all one thing, always had been and always would be. It looked like galaxies, and stars, and planets - a million, a bijillion points of light, millions upon millions of suns - but it was really one thing. In pieces, seemingly. And that one thing was the universal light, the universal being, the Source."

Margaret was on a roll, "No wonder the night sky has held so much fascination, when you think about what you are really looking at. And why heaven is associated with the sky...that sort of thing. Anyway, think about our own sun, without which life as we know it would not be possible, for a million reasons. Because when you really think about it...even when we eat, we are eating sunlight, converted in a myriad way. But, I'm off on a tangent... Am I going on too much?"

"No, no. Never. Never..." Ricky had gone very silent. Very still. But, make no mistake, he was paying attention. Was he ever.

"So even the space, even the dark, was actually made of light. And sound too. All of supposed, or what we call, space - both in the sky, or within the molecules of things, in between the atoms - macrocosm or microcosm - was, and is, actually full. Full of the creative source of all things. That being the case, it is all light. Everything. And nothing but light, light made visible different ways, as if it were concrete. Anyway, there's more about that - a pile more - because, then, it follows that, essentially, we are, each one of us, made of that same starlight, as is everything."

"Incredible..."

"That, of course, is a whole other discussion. Because that makes you a bit of God, and me too. And each and every person, each and every animal, each and every rock and river... Each and every thing! Many people and some religions have recognized this. Jesus and many of the religions in the East. Many other. I remember Joseph Campbell talking about this ..."

Ricky was shaking his head...in agreement. He, too, had read Joseph Campbell. Still, he was a bit in disbelief.

Margaret's train of thought had been derailed. She tried to get back on track.

"In any case, to get back to your original question. When it comes to astrology, to me, it just makes sense that the constellations of light at your time of birth, all part of that grand scheme of things, would very definitely have an effect, in fact, potentially an intense effect, on how you might present, as a person, born under a particular sign of the zodiac. And the best astrologers, the ones who have really studied and know their stuff really well, but who are also extremely intuitive and who in fact can channel an astrological reading for you...well, they seem to be able to be incredibly accurate about a lot of things, sometimes with great amounts of detail."

"Have you written about this?" Ricky asked, somewhat incredulous.

"No, no, not yet..."

"Oh, my God, Margaret, you must. You must. It is phenomenal. Truly it is."

"All in good time, I would imagine. I'm glad you find it interesting..."

"Margaret, this is not just interesting. It has the potential to be...I can't even think of a word big enough. It really does..."

"Actually, there's more...and..."

"More...!? How can there be more? Like what...?"

"It also has come to me that that original light, that original energy, that it always was. Always existed and always will. Well, that that energy continues to exist, exactly - really and truly - as it was and always has been, even before the creation of anything and everything else. That time and space truly are illusions that were created along with duality..."

"And that when we pass from the physical back to the spiritual, that we remember with Spirit again. Kind of like a solid turning into a gas. Except that our essential being has, in truth, always been a gas. It is our soul, our observer, our Spirit-self which resides within our body, our temporary body, which we have perceived as solid, but which is really a light vehicle holding our light essence..." Margaret paused and then went on.

"And that when we die, that we, once more, touch that original energy, that pure love, pure creativity, that pure Source energy. That's what makes us go 'Ahhhhhh...' The light at the end of the tunnel, that great central eternal sun. The pure love, pure bliss, without any of the contrast of duality, without any of the opposite of love - without any fear, any dark, any duality of any kind. The pre-"big-bang" energy as it always was. Always will be. The Great Mystery. Just pure, blissful, indescribable love..."

Margaret took a breath and went on, "People who have had near death experiences often come back from them with an understanding that they need not be so afraid to live...and a pile of other things. They have touched the pre-fear energy..."

"Margherita, you must write this. You must. Have you made notes on all of this? It is almost too much to comprehend..."

"Actually, I haven't. Much of the time, I do, but for some reason, on this topic, I haven't yet."

"It is incredible. Just incredible. How on earth can we go back to talking about mundane things after that? I feel like I have just been told...I don't know...the history of the Universe. You have given me gooseflesh, Margherita. Really, you have."

"Gooseflesh is good," Margaret laughed. Ricky smiled. Margaret continued, thinking she had monopolized the conversation for quite long enough.

"Well, let's just carry on, shall we...? What do you think about horoscopes? Tell me about what you believe in. Are you a Catholic?"

"Naturally, I was brought up Catholic," answered Ricky. "In this country, that is just the way it is...or was, at least... But, as I have aged, I have started to view the world and my beliefs differently. However, I am not an atheist. Not at all. Some people here describe themselves that way now. They have been disillusioned. Or sometimes, they just have not been able to swallow some of the dogma, or, indeed, all of the dogma, of the religion. And, lacking a better explanation, they have chosen to believe in nothing, although that is a bit of an oxymoron - is that the right word? - a contradiction." Margaret nodded.

Ricky continued, "God, as so often depicted in our Art, as a sage old man in the sky, and one that sits in judgement, has, for some, challenged some modern sensibilities. That's why I found what you had to say about sin today so interesting. That and, of course, that you seem to have so many different, thoughtful perspectives on so many things.

"Listen, Margherita, you never did tell me. What sign of the zodiac are you born under?"

"Can you guess?" she asked, smiling.

"Ah," Ricky chortled, knowingly, "I know exactly what it is. I should have realized it immediately. That's why you know so much about Leos, eh? I should have known... Shall we try to outrule one another, do you suppose? Or outcharm? Which do you think?"

"Knowing Leos, probably both, no?" she teased.

And, interestingly enough, Margaret and Ricky argued about things. They argued over the cause of wars, Margaret thinking that at the basis of things - "in fondo" - that most wars were actually religious wars, and Ricky, absolutely disagreeing, saying that wars were about money - power, money, colonization, resources, invasions for economic purposes. Margaret, undaunted, countered that the reason that people couldn't share power, money, land, resources of all kinds was that, deep down inside, the parties saw one another as "the other", the enemy, because their fundamental beliefs were different. Or, so they thought, said Margaret - the ultimate cruel irony. In the end, Margaret and Ricky had to agree to disagree on that one.

And the two of them talked about those resources. How absolutely ridiculous it was to use finite resources of the planet for short-term economic gain.... while the future of the entire planet was at stake. Finite resources. Coal, created when there had been a mass extinction on the planet. Oil, when oceans had dried up and a massive number of fish had died. They would run out one day. Of course, they would. Coal. Oil. Fish. Trees. You name it. How, not only, short-sighted - how moronic! On that, they agreed.

Who was really going to step up and educate people about this? And counteract the propaganda of those who benefitted financially from depleting those finite resources. Bill Moyer had had a great guest, Anthony Leiserowitz, who talked about doing exactly that. And where had she seen that? PBS. The Public Broadcasting System. Again. Home of Wayne Dyer and Shawn Achor and Deepak Chopra and Rudy Tanzi and Mark Walton and Brenda Watson, and a million others. All on the right track. About so many different things. So many.

"I also saw something amazing on the CBC, the Canadian Broadcasting Corporation, on David Suzuki's show, 'The Nature of Things.' Did you know that Ecuador, for example, has granted constitutional rights to Mother Earth, where nature has the right to be respected for its existence and for the maintenance and regeneration of its life cycles? Isn't that absolutely fantastic!? The wisdom of First Nations' peoples all over the planet. It is time we listened to that wisdom. I think it is our salvation..." said Margaret.

"So, ultimately, Margherita, what do you think makes the world go round?" Ricky really wanted to hear the answer.

"Well, no one knows for sure, do they? I have a friend, Pam, back at home, who once said to me that she thought that gravity was love. Gravity, a scientific word which gets used all the time but which really has no explanation, not really. They say it's the force that makes any two objects want to move towards each other."

Margaret smiled and continued, "Well, at home one day, I was watching a television show about the Milky Way, on the Discovery Channel, and as they were talking about the birth of stars and about nebulae, they kept using the phrase, 'but gravity wins.' I had to laugh, out loud really, because gravity makes the world go round, and as we all know, love makes the world go round. Fantastic stuff really...to think that gravity is love. James Bullock is the name of the scientist I remember from that show and the other thing I remember is that some cosmologists believe that all the stars and all the galaxies that we can see represent something like one half of one percent of the mass that seems to be out there. The rest is invisible and mysterious. Of course, it is..." Margaret laughed.

And on and on they went - from spirituality to their respective marriages, both now over; to their children, passions of their lives. Hours had passed when Ricky sked her, "Margherita...?" Just the way he said it was a caress. "Shall we walk a bit and have coffee and dessert later?"

"Oh, yes, please, Ricky, let's walk."

Margaret sought out Roberto before they left. "Mille grazie, a thousand thank yous, Roberto," she said, as she shook his hand. "It was one of the most memorable meals ever!"

"You are so welcome, Miss Gabriel, and so sweet. Please come back as our guest whenever you are able. We hope to see you again soon. ArrivederLa."

Ricky put her wrap around her shoulders and automatically, and quite naturally, lifted her hair so that it would not be caught under the edge of her shawl.

"You look gorgeous," he said. And kissed her again, this time with considerably more heat. He changed the angle of the kiss. When the kiss started, he hadn't been touching her at all, except lips to lips. But, as he changed the angle of the kiss, the intensity changed too, and his hands came up to either side of her face. Margaret couldn't help herself - she kissed him back. She really kissed him back. "Don't stop. Don't stop..." she thought. "May this never end..."

"Mmmm... So nice..." said Ricky, "So very nice... I hope to do a lot more of that, little one. For now, let's walk."

And walk they did. Hand in hand. Arm in arm. Arms around each other. No awkward moments. Or self-consciousness. Ricky was attentive, beyond belief; he was funny. So charming, it hurt. Intellectual. Interesting. Knowledgable. Passionate. Flamboyant. Margaret'd never known anyone like him.

"We won't go to any of the obvious places," he said. "We'll just amble, shall we - is that the right word?"

The night was clear and Rome, at night, like most places, became a different animal. Rome was feline, no doubt. Music, and light and dark, and delicious smells, food and flowers, chestnuts and lively conversations and arguments and laughter. Surrounded by lovers, it was easy to feel like one.

Every once in a while, Ricky would just stop, sometimes mid-sentence, and take her in his arms. It was like living in a story book. Some of those kisses were soft, sweet. Some were ardent, no mistake. Scores of kisses - each one more delicious than the next. He kissed her eyes, her neck, the tip of her nose, just below her ears. Ah...

"You are looking well-kissed, my darling. That makes me happy," he teased. "Would you like that coffee and dessert now?"

"Coffee, yes. Dessert, I don't think so. I just don't have room."

Ricky paid no attention to that, settled her in a chair in an outdoor caffè and ordered coffee, dessert and an after-dinner drink for them. He ordered tartufo for them, the incredible chocolate-mousse-type ice cream, a real confection. One, to share. He fed her the first bite - of course he did. It was unbelievable. It reminded her of something that Elisabetta had said. The first time that Margaret had ever tasted tartufo, she had said, in Italian, to Elisabetta, that it was like an orgasm. Elisabetta, without skipping a beat and with great, straight, perfect delivery, had immediately answered, "Meglio....Better." It was unbelievable - both the dessert and the sensation of being adored and courted or whatever it was that was happening. Seduced, perhaps.

Ricky and Margaret told one another more stories and talked about art, about history, about cars, about their respective struggles with weight, more about their children, about politics, about religion, about spirituality, and, best of all, they laughed. He was funny, incredibly funny, and his face lit up, expressive, animated.

"Let's walk some more," he suggested. "Are you ready to go? Are you tired? You have had a long day."

"Yes, but a beautiful one, a spectacular one. Really, just the best... "

They strolled, very wrapped up in one another, chatting, laughing, sometimes in friendly silence and, in a while, they found themselves outside her hotel. He'd teased her, and charmed her, and surprised her.

They'd stopped and listened to a man playing a concertina. They'd danced. Ricky'd stopped and said, "You are unbelievable. I am the luckiest man in Rome..." And he'd first hummed, then sung in her ear, and whispered, "I believe, Margherita, that I have never met anyone anything like you...not ever." And he'd kissed her, there, in front of everyone, as if no one existed but the two of them. And kissed her again, completely wrapped up in her. And then he'd laughed at her shyness about it, and said, "Dai, Margherita, come on, Margherita..." as if it was the most natural thing in the world, to embrace, extremely intimately, in the beautiful piazzas and vias of one of the most beautiful cities in the world.

"I hope you will agree to see me again. Will you? Will you be in Rome for a while? No? Somewhere else then?"

Ricky'd kissed her one last time. It lasted a very long time - went on and on.

He was an absolute gentleman. She wasn't at all sure if that impressed her or bothered her.

"Buona notte, tesoro. Good night, my darling. Sogni d'oro. Dreams of gold. You will see me, won't you? May I call you?"

She nodded. How could she do anything else?

*****

The next day, outside Margaret's hotel window, right outside her window, on the cobbled street, was someone playing the - what was that? - the violin? Yes, it was the violin. A violin sonata of some sort and the violinist was looking right up at her and nodding, smiling. She shivered with delight. By the end, the tears ran freely down her face. It had been

- exquisite - absolutely, unforgettably exquisite. The violinist bowed deeply and disappeared.

At the hotel desk, there was a card that had been delivered for her.


Tesoro. Darling.

Roses couldn't express. Only an experience would do. May you remember it always. Indimenticabile - unforgettable - like you.

Tanti baci, so many kisses,
Ricky


So, okay, he was good. Damned good.




Listen to" I Love You (Ti amo)"
by Andre Rieu

# Thank God for Red Shoes

## Chapter 7 - The Superego

Under ideal conditions, an ego filled to the brim will push down into the superego - the home of ultimate love, ultimate good and peace. Your ego motivates your personality to listen to your superego. This is the good angel talking on your shoulder.

A person fulfilling a part of her or his mission is able to access a sense of joy. A sense of accomplishment grows down into a sense of unity. The sense of separation thins. Acceptance grows. Resistance weakens. Love grows. Fear weakens. Unity grows. Isolation diminishes. Stillness grows. Noise diminishes. Self-love permits endless love. Recognition of our eternal sacred essence astounds and humbles us. Recognition of our miraculous sensory experiential ability does the same. Love and acceptance.

Love and acceptance.

We've touched peace. Peace, I tell you.

The superego is the home of the most extreme forms of love.

The superego is affiliated with the respiratory system.

Breathing is an amazing exchange of energy. In goes oxygen, out comes carbon dioxide. In goes positive energy. Out comes negative energy.

The trees, our planet's lovely own set of lungs, take in carbon dioxide an expel oxygen. Wow!!! What a system! What an amazingly balanced system.

We breathe out. They take it in. They breathe out. We take it in.

And, so many have pondered, "Should we be amputating our lungs?"

Is it possible that Source energy is right here in our air? Can it be that inhaling is filling our being with Spirit, with inspiration, with creativity, infinite patience and endless love? "Take a deep, cleansing breath." We hear it again and again.

As well as exhaling deeply, along with such things as sighing, which is an automatic exhalation of negative energy, we should be sure to inhale deeply to drink in positive energy.

When you feel stressed, try breathing deeply. Walking. Yoga. Biking. Meditation. Andrew Weil, has a great breathing exercise. Read about it in his book, "Eight Weeks to Optimum Health." (11)

Breathing is the ultimate balancing act. And, if we've learned anything, it's that balance is good.

# Capitolo Otto

Listen to "Un Muso Duro"
by Italia loves Emilia

"I can't walk that way," Margaret thought. "I just can't do it. Don't want to do it." Back in Venice, Margaret could not bring herself to walk through the two columns in the piazzetta, the little piazza that led from the water's edge to Piazza San Marco. Couldn't. The two columns had been there forever, right at the entrance of the city, right in front of the Palazzo Ducale, the Doge's Palace, standing on guard, in welcome, in warning also perhaps.

Once, many years ago, before they had cordoned the columns off, Margaret had tried to sit on the base of one of them, but had found that she just couldn't stay. At the time, she wasn't sure why. Now, she knew. On the top of one of the columns was perched, San Marco, Saint Mark, patron saint of Venice and on top of the other, San Teodoro, Saint Theodore. San Marco, the patron saint of Venice. San Teodoro, the patron saint of Venice before Saint Mark's relics were brought to Venice in 828.

And Margaret wasn't alone. Many people won't walk in between them, those two columns. They just won't do it. And there's a reason why...why not.

People used to be hung there. Right between the two columns. On public display. Many people. Many. And burned. Uuuuhf...it gave her shivers.

Margaret had no doubt whatsoever that at some point in the past she too had been burned there. She could smell the smoke, feel the flames.

It was terrifying. They had said she was a witch...a strega; a woman with some kind of intuitive powers; a woman who healed; a woman who had visions; a woman, who must be of the devil. Must be. The horrible heat, the sensation in her feet, the horror, the smell of her own flesh starting to roast... The sensation was so horrific, she couldn't stay and remember it. She just couldn't. And, whenever Margaret walked between those two columns, those two stupendous columns - powerful or innocuous, depending on your point of view - all the sensations started to come to her again. Memory of place. Had it always been this way? Had it?

*****

Margaret, who didn't really have a church at home, nonetheless attended church almost every Sunday while she was Italy. She had sat in churches and attended mass all over the country. She also would sometimes go in just to sit. She found it a great place to meditate. Margaret had decided to go and sit at the back of San Zaccaria, a church she just loved. She wasn't the only one to love it. It was loved by many. Elton John and his partner, David, had named their baby boy Zachary, that very church in mind.

And to top it off, years ago, Margaret had had one of those flashback moments when she remembered being there at another time. Time... And space... Ai, yiai, yiai. She had had a Shirley MacLaine moment - a moment of real insight - a real sense of knowing. And God bless Shirley, who had had the guts to tell her truth, regardless of the ridicule, the ribbing, the reputation she had had to endure. Margaret had remembered living there, in that very Venetian neighbourhood. Right there. It felt somewhat like deja vu. But there was no doubt. She even knew what her name had been. She had lived there before. A few times. It was all coming back.

*****

It was time for dance circle again. Elisabetta couldn't go this time...had to spend time with a cousin that was visiting, a cousin she hadn't seen for years. She and Margaret had made plans to meet up later at the bar. Margaret had a magnificent time as she always did.

Michele said to her, "I have a surprise for you."

"You do?" Margaret asked, surprised already.

"Yes, will you come over to my house? It isn't far from here."

"Okay..."

"When dancing is finished, we will go?"

"Okay..."

Michele lived in a beautiful building, literally just around the corner from the school where they went dancing. They went up thousands of steps, he opened the door, and ushered Margaret in.

There, in his living room, what else but a tent, a tent made of beautiful oriental blankets!

"Not terribly original," Michele confessed, "but lots of fun to put together. Come see." Inside, enchantment. A million cushions, all in jewel tones - ruby red, sapphire, emerald, topaz, amethyst, gold - and, in Italian mason jars, the kind they put homemade ragu in, tiny candles everywhere. He lit them.

"Oh, my God, Michele, it is amazing! Just amazing!" Margaret was enchanted.

"Come in. Sit down. I have Prosecco ready."

Margaret shook her head. It was unbelievable. So sweet. Really, sweet. And, as Michele returned with the Prosecco and two flutes, she realized that he had put on a CD. It was "La Traviata" - the only Italian opera she had ever seen. The opening refrains always brought her to tears. It was so heart-breakingly beautiful, so delicate, so poignant that it hurt. She'd always thought of it as quintessentially Italian. By the time they got to "Libiamo", the happy drinking song, Margaret had really started to relax.

Listen to the "Overture from 'La Traviata'"

"I've made us some dinner - I hope you don't mind..."

"Mind?! I'm famished. What have you made?"

"Tagliatelle ai fruiti di mare. Egg noodles with seafood sauce."

"Oh, my God, that is perfect. Perfect."

When Michele reappeared, a while later, with two steaming bowls, Margaret was fairly drooling. The pasta was amazing. Piping hot; shrimps, clams and white fish; cream sauce, delicately flavoured with thyme and lemon, and drizzled over it, a touch of "peperoncino" or "olio santo", as it was sometimes called. "Sacred oil", infused with hot red peppers. It was stupendous.

"This is one of the best things I have ever eaten," Margaret crooned.

"I have to complete the scenario," Michele said, as he pulled out a small leather-bound book, "even if it is stolen from another." It was "Promessi Sposi", "The Betrothed".

"You might want to sit back. Please be comfortable." And with that, he began to read a passage to her - what's more, he was reading to her...in Italian!

Margaret's heart stood still for a second. It was just the sweetest thing ever. Not just sweet - "sweet" was too mushy a sentiment. She was just touched beyond belief - and beside herself with sheer delight. How on earth did she deserve such a life as this?

When he'd finished - silence. Then, after a while, "Oh Michele, it's just beautiful. Truly beautiful. I can't thank you enough, for the whole experience. Really, I don't have enough words. Non ho parole."

"Ohe, Marghe, I am so pleased you like it. It was an absolute pleasure, I can assure you."

After a brief pause, Michele continued, "Listen, Margherita, I have to go to Milan for a couple of days - a chefs' conference, you know."

"Oh, really, Milan? Beautiful, incredible place... I've always found it a bit overwhelming, I must admit."

"It is a stupendous city. Davvero. It really is. But, on the way back, I was thinking of spending a day or two in Liguria, maybe the Cinque Terre. Since the floods, they have been trying to rebuild, but they are the most charming villages, and it is good to support them. Tourism suffered a little, you know."

A year and a half ago, 20 inches of rain had fallen on the area in a really short amount of time. A part of the hills above had collapsed and the flooded two of the five towns really badly, virtually burying the ground-level stores and restaurants and living behind a mountain of mud, five or six feet deep in some places. Lives had been lost. Two of the towns, the two at sea level, Vernazza and Monterossa al Mare, had been completely devastated and both had had to be rebuilt.

"Yes, I know. I've been there. I do love them, all of them. And, you know, I was there, just a week before that horrific landslide. It was devastating. I was so worried about everyone there."

"Yes, it was a tragedy, really," Michele answered. "They have worked very hard to rebuild. They were without electricity or services for a long while. But they have been very successful with their efforts to begin again. Well, in any case, I wondered if you might like to join me. I have a favourite hotel in Monterosso, and I could book some rooms for us. We could hike up the trails, or sit on the beach, or drink Prosecco sitting in the sun - or all of those things... What do you say? Che cosa ne pensi?"

"I say it sounds just...so idyllic, really."

"I have a chef friend there who will make us the most amazing dinner. You will see!"

"I'd better check about the dates..."

"Next weekend. For Friday night and Saturday morning. I could meet you in Monterossa, at the train station. Do you think you are free?"

"I think so but I'd better double check. Oh, that sounds just so relaxing – perfect really."

"I am glad you think so..."

"And, look, I'm so sorry, Michele, but I really must go. I don't want to go. It's been one of the best evenings ever. But, I must..."

"Do not worry, Margherita. Shall I walk you back to your apartment?"

"No, thank you, Michele, but I'm supposed to be meeting Elisabetta at the bar – I should just run. Thank you - so much - really - for everything."

"Ah, Margherita, you are most welcome. And I know how punctual you Canadians like to be. Ci vediamo. See you." Michele kissed Margaret's cheeks and she was on her way.

*****

"Oh, my God," said Margaret to Elisabetta. "That was just unbelievable. He went to all that trouble - it was incredible. I just can't get over it."

"Ah," uttered Elisabetta, knowingly, "I think your Michele may be somewhat smitten with you, wouldn't you say?"

"No! No...we don't have that kind of relationship. We just don't. We dance. We talk. We talk a lot. We're friends..."

"You may not now. But, listen, I know Italian men. If it's not a romance now, it won't be long before it becomes one. Plus, you'd told him it was sexy, no? Wasn't the word you used?"

"No, Elisabetta, you're just crazy. It's not like that. It just isn't..." Maybe it wasn't the best time to mention the Cinque Terre... Hmmm...

"You think not, eh?" smiled Elisabetta.

*****

The next day Margaret was back in their apartment, painting, trying to capture the sky. Di was out somewhere. Margaret's Italian cell phone rang.

"Pronto," she answered. That's how Italians answered the phone, by saying that they were ready.

"Margherita, sono io. It is I...Ricky."

"Oh, how nice to hear from you, Ricky. How have you been?"

"Excellent, thank you. Listen, Margherita, the show has aired and the response is through the roof."

"Really?"

"Yes, really. Book sales seem to be up too."

"That's amazing..."

And there's something else," Ricky chuckled. "Something that will make you laugh...it's about red shoes."

"What is it?" Margaret couldn't imagine.

"People are starting to buy up every red shoe they can put their hands on. Isn't that phenomenal!? You, my darling, are a phenomenon..."

"Ricky, you're so sweet."

"I am not sweet, but you are. Dolcezza fatta donna. It doesn't translate very well, does it, but luckily you understand what I mean...sweetness masquerading as a woman." Margaret smiled.

"Margherita, congratulations. My darling, I would like to come to see you in Venice. May I?"

"Yes, yes, certainly..." When it rains, it pours...was all that Margaret could think.

"Is next Friday okay, not this one but the next?" This coming weekend she was going to the Cinque Terre, but she was free the weekend after that.

She hesitated. "Yes, that's fine."

"Great. I will take a room at the Danielli. Will you come and meet me there?"

"Yes, sure."

"Great. I'll see you on Friday, then, I should be there by 4pm."

"I'll be there. And Ricky...?"

"Si, tesoro. Yes, darling."

"Thank you."

"The pleasure is all mine. See you soon. Ciao, ciao."

*****

"Look at those shoes!!! Aren't they astounding!?" Margaret asked Di, with enthusiasm. Italy was a shoe-lover's dream and Venice was no exception.

Margaret remembered fondly. "When I first came here, that first time, I bought a pair of shoes. You know, I'd forgotten, but they were red!!! They actually were red. Isn't that crazy? I loved those things. The softest leather. All straps. Bright, beautiful, deep red. I wore them and wore them and finally, sadly, they fell apart, totally beyond repair. You know what? I think it's time for a new pair."

"Well, buddy," chuckled Di, "buy them while you can. There's something in the air and, by the feel of things, there may just be a run on red shoes..."

Listen to "Somewhere Over the Rainbow"
by Ariane Moffat

## Chapter 8 - The Supershadow

Underneath the shadow is the supershadow. This is the home of the most extreme forms of fear. It is the home of the darkest of the dark. The home of rage, of violence, of revenge, of crime, of ruthlessness, of evil, the urge to harm or kill others, to kill yourself. This is the black demon on your shoulder. It's the one talking to you telling you it might be thrilling to shoplift something. It's the one telling you it might be the answer to your extreme unhappiness and depression if you just ended it all.
And worse.


We all have it - but in deep dark recesses and for most of us, we don't see it or feel it much.

If your shadow is really full, with no relief, it has to go somewhere. It can stimulate the ego to get bigger and work harder to try to cancel it out. Sometimes that just doesn't work. Sometimes, the shadow just has too much stuff in it or the ego too little, or both.

Sometimes, it has nowhere to go but to seep down towards the supershadow, eliciting our darkest sides.

People who have experienced unfathomable amounts of abuse of various kinds have sometimes had their shadows so filled with negative energies that they find themselves, through no fault of their own, touching their supershadows.

> A. Gilligan, in his book, "Our Deadly Epidemic and its Causes", writes, "I have yet to see a serious act of violence that was not provoked by the experience of feeling shamed and humiliated, disrespected and ridiculed, and that did not represent the attempt to prevent or undo this 'loss of face' - no matter how severe the punishment, even if it includes death." (12)

Shame is one of the lowest energies there is.

The supershadow is affiliated with the genitals, although, obviously, not all violence has to do with the genitals.

Sex is a sacred, wondrous thing. It takes you very close to unity, to bliss, to Spirit energy.

But when this sacred thing is turned inside out by being used as a tool for domination and control, all hell breaks loose.

The use of the genitals as a tool of violence is the ultimate sacrilege.

The victims of sexual abuse sometimes turn into abusers themselves. Their shadows have been filled so much because of someone's supershadow that they touch their own supershadow.

Sometimes, rather than that, they withdraw, as if they were leaving their bodies - but they often are left with debilitating residue, not being able to trust - not others, but even worse, not

themselves. They have very full shadows, often
directed at themselves and can end up spending a
lot of their lives in the shade - in depression,
in disease.

The misuse of genitals in control and violence
is hell.

# Capitolo Nove

Listen to "Insieme Finire" by Biagio Antonacci

Michele had told Margaret that he would meet her at the train station in Monterosso. She had always enjoyed that train trip from Venice to the Italian Riviera, especially the part of the trip where one travelled through long sections in dark tunnels, through the mountains and cliffs and then - suddenly - shockingly - every time, shockingly, even though you were expecting it - that wild burst into the sunshine and visual blast of the incredible sea. Then, plunged back into darkness. Then, another shot of the coast, the sea foaming. Then another. A tease of what was to come.

Margaret had first come here many years ago, with a girlfriend, to Camogli, a charming seaside village, and had adored it. The smell of the sea; the first time she had eaten real focaccia, perfumed, "profumata", they said, with the sweetest onions ever; the fishermen's catch; the cats; light-as-a-cloud 'trofie', the traditional pasta of Liguria, little twisted gnocchi, in the greenest, most fragrant pesto ever; the steep, sometimes gruelling trails, worth every minute of tired legs and vertigo, both.

She was almost there.

No funny business on the train. She had learned, the hard way, the results of riding the train without first validating the ticket at the little machines, that somehow never seemed to work properly anyway, at the train station. A fine, that's what you got, even if you pleaded tourist ignorance. Well, not this time.

First Riomaggiore, then Manarola, closer and closer, then Corniglia, then beloved Vernazza, and then, chug, chug, chug into Monterosso. The double doors opened and down she hopped.

At first Margaret couldn't see Michele. And then, there he was, looking quite gorgeous, with the wind ruffling his hair slightly.

"Margherita, here I am..."

And then he was in front of her, with the traditional greeting, kissing her on each cheek.

"How wonderful you..." Margaret started to say.

But, Michele was looking at her in the strangest way, and suddenly said, "Oh, fuck it." And with that, he took her face very slowly between his two beautiful hands and kissed her, slowly and very firmly, on the mouth, deepening that kiss, that rapturous kiss. He smelled of aftershave and coffee and of freshly-pressed shirt. Clean and masculine, and sexy - so sexy. She really hadn't thought of him that way before, not really. But this, this, well, this was something different.

He pulled away slightly. "Have I offend..."

"Sh..." she said. What the hell was happening? Here he was, looking absolutely gorgeous, and smelling of sunshine, like freshly dried sheets, and somehow, wicked. Michele? Wicked? And he was looking at her like... like... Oh, what the hell... What the hell...

And then Margaret smiled, a little shyly, "Can we do that again, do you think?" She surprised herself. Where the hell had that come from? It sounded just like Carmen Diaz talking to Jude Law in "The Holiday." What the hell was she doing?

Michele's smile suddenly reappeared, bright as the Ligurian sun. "Thank God...Oh yes, yes, we can, indeed."

Again, it being Italy, no one paid them any attention as they stood locked in embrace, kissing again and again.

She broke away, "I am not, however, going to bed with you. Not under any circumstances..."

Michele laughed out loud at that, looking remarkably like Rhett Butler at the moment, his dimples, his fossette, deepening. "Of course, you aren't!" he said. "That would never do, would it?"

"Oh, give me your arm, and let's walk," urged Margaret. "I refuse to let anything complicate my time here. I absolutely refuse, do you hear? We are just going to take it all very easy."

"Oh, Margherita, you are adorable. Dolcissima. The sweetest."

He took her bag in one hand and her arm in the other. "You're going to love this hotel. It is truly magnificent. And the people are wonderful, old friends, in fact." Inside, Margaret was both tickled pink and somewhat confused simultaneously. "What the hell am I going to do now?" she wondered. Was it fair to him? Crap, was it fair to her? And what about Ricky? Shit.

In an instant she decided. She would do exactly what Scarlett O'Hara would do. She would think about it tomorrow.

*****

Michele and Margaret set out for dinner arm in arm. As they walked through the tunnel on the way to the Old Town, the Centro, the guy with the keyboard was playing at the entrance, as he often did. Margaret and Michele had a quick spin, while he played. So much fun.

They had the most memorable dinner at Michele's friend's restaurant in Monterosso. Seafood stew, served from an urn, an amfora, and upturned at the table into a huge bowl - served over garlic bruschetta, placed in the bottom of each individual diner's dinner bowl. It was all the things memories are made of. They smiled. They laughed. They had so much fun. Pure delight.

As they walked back to their hotel, it started to rain. Really rain. Hard. Thunder. Luckily, they had an umbrella, Margaret's favourite red umbrella, and they walked fairly quickly as the rain really started to pelt. It was turning into the most spectacular Ligurian thunderstorm, "temporale", with lightning lustily kissing the sky and thunder rolling and reverberating across the mountains.

"Will you join me for a hot drink? Some tea, or perhaps, a "digestivo", an afterdinner drink?" asked Michele.

"Yes, please. I feel chilled to the bone," answered a shivering Margaret.

Michele ordered room service. The scalding tea felt great. Super hot. Margaret sipped it, wrapped her hands around the cup. Michele reached out and took the cup from her hands, putting it down on the coffee table.

"Here you are, looking so desirable. I just can't resist." Michele took her in his arms and kissed her - kissed her as though he loved her already, and had for an eternity. The thunder rolled. She kissed him back. And, it hit her. Oh...oh... Oh, she had known him! She had loved him! Oh, my God! And here they were...reunited...

They fell into bed - the easiest, most natural thing in the world. It just happened...

Much later, Michele, looking adoringly at Margaret, said, "You are the most stunning creature, really. You are sunlight - moonlight - sometimes you are candlelight. Oh, God, I want you so much," he said, kissing her eyes, her forehead, her face. "I've just had you and I want you again."

After a long while, just as the sun was coming up, "Again..." said Margherita sleepily, "again..."

"You are insatiable, you know, my darling. Thank God for it..." And the morning sun burst through the window, basking the two lovers in pale golden Ligurian morning light and casting their shadows on the wall as they moved again as one.

# Capitolo Dieci

Listen to "Pensami" by Julio Iglesias

The week went by slow-fast. Michele had to be away from Venice again, something to do with work, off to buy wine for the restaurant. They had  spoken on the phone, though, a couple of times. Such a lovely man. Margaret considered herself very fortunate. She and Di went to do one of the book signings, in Verona. There was a pile of people there. Many more than expected. The next thing Margaret knew; it was Friday again. Time for Ricky.

*****

Margaret had never been into the Danielli. By it, many times - many - but, in it, never. The lobby was something else. Gorgeous. Understated and ostentatious at the same time. Very posh. What else could one expect? It was the Danieli.

The magnificent-looking person at the desk looked up, "Buona sera. Good afternoon. Ah, Miss Gabriel, il Signore Delvecchio is expecting you. He said to go right up. The elevator is just there. Suite 1111. Shall I accompany you?"

"No, no," Margaret couldn't help but laugh out loud a little. "I'll make my way, but grazie tanto, thank you so much," she answered.

Margaret knocked lightly at the door.

Ricky opened the door. Fabulously-dressed as always, his smile broadened. "Ah, bellissima Margherita. You are more and more stunning every time I see you. Let me look at you properly." He held her out at the end of his arms to have a look at her, and then, after shaking his head in disbelief as if to say "How can you be real?", he brought her in close to kiss her, first on the left cheek and then on the right.

"As are you Ricky. As are you... What an amazing room! What an amazing view!" Margaret couldn't help herself. She went to the window, and there, at her feet, lay the lagoon. San Giorgio Maggiore. And vaporetti. And gondolas. And the lagoon itself, lapping, lapping. And traghetti. Ferries. And the beautiful sleek, wooden water taxis. Blues and greys and a million shades of pearl. And Vivaldi. And Marco Polo. And Giorgione. And Casanova. All echoing off the walls.

"How magnificent is that? It takes my breath away, you know, every time. It is just never the same twice, is it?" Margaret never ceased to be in awe.

"There's no place like it. It casts its spell... It's not for everyone, as you know. However, if you like it, if it gets immediately into your bones, you won't just like it. Venezia doesn't tolerate 'like'. It just won't. It's love or nothing, in Venezia. You either adore it or you hate it. There doesn't seem to be much middle ground with Venezia. Like all places, or people, in fact, with strong personalities..."

He had music on. What was that? Margaret knew it, but couldn't place it.

"Margherita, I took the liberty of ordering tea. I thought it might remind you of your beloved British Columbia."

"Ricky, how wonderful! And how sweet of you. Look at it. It is unbelievable."

The tea tray, a tiered plate, was complete with tramezzini, the teeny triangular sandwiches which tasted like nothing else on earth - it was Italian mayonnaise that made the difference, she was convinced; perfect, tiny scones with cream and strawberry preserves; zeppole, little cream puffs; a couple of chocolate confections; and all of it decorated beautifully with edible flowers - violas, and rose petals and cornflowers.

And of course, a silver tea service with steaming hot Earl Grey tea, which the Italians seemed to have adopted as their own, always served clear, with lots of lemon juice, slices of lemon and an inordinate amount of sugar. When she had first had it that way, she had not enjoyed it. But Elisabetta had made it for her that way a million times now, and no one made a cup of tea like Elisabetta. Margaret had become a convert.

Now, she recognized the music. It was André Rieu. From that indescribable concert in Cortona, the one she had seen on PBS, on KPTS, from Seattle. André Rieu had also been taken hostage by the charms of Italy and, with his brother, had actually composed the most incredible love song to Cortona. It had all the musical qualities that Margaret identified as quintessentially Italian - lyrical, and delicate, and bittersweet, and powerful and tender, and magnificent.

Margaret loved that concert, loved everything about it. Loved André; loved the beautiful dresses that all of the women in his orchestra wore, each in a different colour, each in a different style; loved the playful way the members of the orchestra interacted with one another; loved the incredible violin in his incredible hands; loved the response of the audience; loved the music itself; the rapport that André had with his fellow musicians and his audience members; loved his absolute charisma. Actually, in that, André and Ricky shared a lot.

"So, my darling, what have you been doing?"

"Oh, Ricky, I've been having the best time. I've been walking, and dancing, a lot, in fact, and visiting all my favourite places, and discovering new ones. And reading, a pile, and writing. Actually, I've been writing a lot."

"Have you written the notes about what we were talking about in Rome?"

"Yes, I have started to try to record all that. But, you know, it has a life of its own. And a time of its own. One day I'll just wake up and realize that it's time to write it. It just goes like that. How about you? What have you been up to?"

"Ah, work mostly. I have this new show, you know. Yes, of course, you know, and it's taking up most of my time..." He stopped. A slow smile came over his face.

"Come here... Vieni qua..." said Ricky, very, very quietly, but sounding serious.

"Ricky...?" queried Margaret. What was he up to?

"Come here..." he said, more convincingly this time, and with a more dangerous look in his eye.

"Ricky, you're not going to tell me what to do," said Margaret, thinking back on their conversation about who was going to rule whom. And, smiling back, in spite of herself, but determined not to let the Italian-male thing overwhelm her.

"I'm not telling you what to do," he said, very sincerely, and then his grin got bigger. "I want you to have your way with me. Kiss me," he encouraged. "Come on..."

"Ricky..." Suddenly, the memory of Michele got strong. Very strong.

"Kiss me," Ricky repeated, in his inimitable way, part dare, part delight.

In spite of herself, Margaret laughed. Okay, so she'd humour him. Not that it was so difficult. It was just a kiss. No big deal. She walked over to him and stood in front of him. She bent over and, very quietly, very softly, kissed him on the lips. She pulled away.

"Like you mean it. Convince me," he laughed intimately, his voice deep and husky. Ricky was irresistible. Totally irresistible.

"Oh, what the hell..." thought Margaret. And she was lost. Again. It was bigger than her. And with that, she did exactly what she wanted to do. Margaret lowered herself, very gently, onto his lap, wrapped her hands around his head, holding his beautiful head with her fingers just in his hair behind his ears, and kissed him, really kissed him, in earnest. Suddenly, she was the one trying to seduce him. She wanted to feel that power over him. She deepened the kisses.

"Baciami. Baciami. Kiss me. Kiss me," Ricky whispered, as Margaret stopped for a minute and then began again, now completely intoxicated.

In the background now, Julio Iglesias was singing. In Italian. What was he singing? "Pensami...Think of me. Sognami...Dream of me. Baciami...kiss me. Si puo arrivare alle stelle.... We can go to the stars..."

Margaret was kissing Ricky's neck. She felt bold. She did exactly what she wanted to do. She loosened his tie the better to drop kisses on his neck. She felt deliciously out of control and in control all at once.

"Vuoi andare alle stelle, Margherita? Do you want to go to the stars?" Ricky asked, suggestively, yes, but with such tenderness, gentleness. "Oh, so poetic. So romantic..." she thought. Another rush of hormones, felt instantly. And then, in rapid succession, "Oh, shit. That kind of go to the stars."

The song was ending. Julio was singing, "Si puo andare alle stelle...it is possible to go to the stars. Dicendo...semplicemente... sì. By simply... saying...yes." All sung, with perfect...pregnant... pauses.

"We're not going to do that... No, no, no. We're not." said Margaret, smiling weakly, with more than a little regret, but trying to sound serious. Relieved too. She felt relieved.

"Aah... We are already doing that..." Ricky observed with a wry but satisfied smile, and quite rightly.

His hands... Oh, his hands... He had the most magnificent hands.

"Ricky... I'm tempted...I'm not going to lie. I am. But..." A long slow 'but'. "But tempted as I am..."

"You know what we Italians say about temptation - 'Everything in moderation except temptation.' Temptation, you should go for..." Ricky smiled that infuriatingly charming smile.

"I've never heard that expression..."

"You couldn't have. I just made it up," he laughed, lightening the mood, but not the heat.

"You're bad. So bad." The bad boy thing.

"Look, we're both adults," responded Ricky. "I think you are incredibly smart, creative, inspired. You're intuitive beyond belief, gorgeous. Independent and strong, yet extremely feminine, not to mention very, very sexy - all simultaneously. As well, you are altruistic, thoughtful, and absolutely opinionated. Argumentative, even - which I love. You are one of the most brilliant people I know...truly brilliant. Inside and out. 'Solare,' we say in Italian. Like the sun. Radiant. So much light emanates from you. Everyone feels it. You have only to walk into a room, and if someone had their head down, they would think that someone had just opened the shutters and let in the sunshine. And, here you are looking so delicious, as you always do. I really do want to kiss you everywhere. I do..."

"Oh, Ricky... It's just too early. That's all..."

"Too early in the day, you mean?" asked Ricky innocently, deliberately misunderstanding, the little monkey. "Believe me, it is not too early. I want to make love to you in the daylight, in the moonlight. On the water. Outside, in a field of flowers. In candlelight. On the beach. At daybreak. As the sun is setting. In the evening, just before dusk, when the light is magical, and bathes everything in gold..." He tucked her hair behind her ear and kissed the tip of her nose. Everything the man said sounded like poetry.

"No, not too early in the day. You know, damn well, that's not what I mean," Margaret laughed, in spite of her self. "Too early in the relationship. Look,  let's get out of here. You're much too hard to resist and it's not a good idea. And, besides..."

"Sh, sh, amore, love, be quiet," Ricky said, but very kindly, softly, good-naturedly, as he placed his finger, extremely gently, over her lips. "Lasciamo perdere. Let's drop it. For now... But you know, Margherita, it is not going to go away, this thing between us. We have this most amazing thing between us. It is intoxicating. It is not just chemistry either. You too know that it is more than that by now – although there is chemistry also - in spades, I believe you say. I want you. I do. No doubt about that. Never doubt. I want you, and only you. In the worst way. In many ways, in fact, infatti." He was incorrigible. "Make no mistake, Margherita, the stars are in our future. They are... It's just a matter of timing. We will get there, you'll see, I am certain of it," he laughed.

"Incorrigible..." Margaret repeated, ever so fondly, as Ricky silenced her with another heady kiss. "And totally irresistible..." she thought.

*****

Ricky and Margaret went for a long, wonderful walk and ended up going to dinner, deep in the centre of Venice. The water sparkled; the moon rose.

"What are you up to in the next little while?" wondered Ricky.

"In the next couple of weeks? Well, I have a book signing in Sorrento. We are go into stay in Positano, I think, because I have friends there. And I am getting ready for a speech in Florence..."

"When will you be in Positano?"

"Soon, week after next."

"If my schedule allows it, could we meet up for the day there? Maybe you and Di and I could do some things together?"

"That sounds nice. It really does."

As Ricky walked Margaret back to her apartment, they decided to walk through Piazza San Marco, even though they didn't have to. Just to go and listen to the orchestras for a minute. There were always a million people in the Piazza and, also, always in the background, the lingering aroma of spaghetti sauce. And gamberetti, shrimp, perhaps. And was that white wine...? And, always, the salty scent of the sea.

All the orchestras were playing, each from their respective corner of the piazza. The musicians, in formal dress, seemed from another era. Tuxedos and long dresses, so wonderful, and, in her mind, now, so Venetian. So often, those poor musicians looked bored to death, playing the same tunes day after day, night after night. Duelling Venetian orchestras, can you imagine anything better? Or worse? But the musicians tonight at Quadri seemed pretty animated. Not burnt out at all. They were playing lots of popular American songs, from the forties and fifties especially, and a few Italian things here and there, but they were smiling, almost as if they were having fun.

> "I'm gonna sit right down and write myself a letter
> And make believe it came from you
> I'm gonna write things oh so sweet
> It's gonna knock me off my feet,
> Kisses on the bottom, I'll be glad I got 'em"

Listen to "I'm Gonna Sit Right Down and Write Myself a Letter" by Paul McCartney and listen to "Al Di La" - from Rome Adventure with Troy Donahue and Suzanne Pleshette

Ricky sang along. He extended his hand. And then took her is his arms. There she was dancing - with Ricky, no less - in Piazza San Marco. How good did life get? The two of them were dancing, together - unbelievably - under the Venetian stars and under the watchful gaze of the Basilica and the Campanile in Piazza San Marco...witnesses, all, to an unfolding, a physical and yet somehow, somewhat mystical unfolding.

At one point, Ricky took Margaret's right hand, which he had been holding out in the traditional dance hold, and changed the position of his hand, wrapping it around hers, changing the angle of their arms and bringing her arm in closer to their bodies, almost in between them, dramatically increasing the sensation of intimacy as they danced and enfolding her somehow. With Ricky, she often felt close to... "swooning", was the only world she think of, although that was so old fashioned. This, for some inexplicable reason, was one of those times...in response to this seemingly-small but very self-assured gesture of intimacy.

"Mmm... What is that scent that you wear always?" Ricky asked.

"Oh, it's French Lace. My Mum first gave me some when I was thirteen and I loved it. I've been wearing it since."

"It undoes me every time. It is how I imagine heaven must smell..."

"Okay, that's it," she thought to herself. "I have died and gone to heaven..." Although, out loud, she just laughed a little and shook her head at him.

Margaret tried to retain her composure. "Actually, they've stopped producing it. To my horror. I went everywhere and bought up every last drop I could find. I'm not sure what I will do when its all used up. I shall have to find a new scent, never easy. It has kind of been my signature scent all of my adult life. I've been looking, but I haven't found the new scent yet. Still looking..."

"Well, it's beautiful. Mmm, even better when you dance..."

"Why don't people who are married say things like that to one another?" Margaret mused aloud. "There would definitely be more oomph...that's for sure..."

Ricky threw his head back at that and laughed that deep, wonderful laugh. "You are so right, my adorable Margherita... So right. Time and familiarity, sometimes the death of romance, no?"

"Not just sometimes. Almost always..." she lamented. "Such a pity. But I guess that's just how it is."

"Perhaps it need not be. I keep hoping, in any case. I hope that you keep hoping also... One must, you know."

Ultimately, that's what everyone wished for. To keep the magic, the sensation of being completely, totally, head-over-heels in love with someone and with life itself, while developing a long-term relationship, with the comfort of companionship, a life shared, a relationship that grew through the years of disagreements and challenges - some big, some small - and of "I'm sorry"s. A witness to one's life, an intimate witness, just as they talked about in "Shall We Dance?" with Richard Gere, Susan Sarandon, and Jennifer Lopez.

Or was it?

And, was it even possible? There was a part of her that longed to find out.

Listen to "Dancing with Cupid"
by Daniel Powter

# Thank God for Red Shoes

## Chapter 9 - The Shade

Excessive negative energies that supersaturate the shadow have to go somewhere and start being pushed towards the supershadow. However, there appears to be a built-in mechanism to avoid sending you into supershadow, unless its absolutely necessary.

Often, those excess energies bulge outwards into a coping mechanism - the Shade - darker than the shadow but not the darkest of dark like the Supershadow. The Supershadow is about extreme cases.

The Shade, instead, is the place of denial, of depression, of repression, of negative energies turned inwards. It's the place of illness.

Negative energies, when spilling over in the direction of the Supershadow, often bulge into the Shade. The sheer volume and/or intensity of negative energies opens a kind of release valve, designed to get your attention to tell that you are out of balance.

If you have too much "negative" energy, it simply needs dissipation or expression. It has to be released or it builds up and up somewhere and finds expression as something else. Often, that something else is dis-ease.

If you don't listen to the clues the Universe is giving you - dissatisfaction, sadness, unhappiness - the message gets louder. And how do you know what underlies the disease? Check with Louise Hay. She can give you clues as to the underlying shadow energies that are creating your situation. Children who come into the world with disease have been exposed to negative energies to an extreme enough extent that they have assimilated them. (13)

The Shade is affiliated with the pancreas. The word pancreas comes from the Greek words meaning "all" and "flesh". (14)

The pancreas secretes digestive enzymes into the small intestine and it also is a gland that produces several important hormones including insulin, glucagon and somatostatins. Interestingly enough, the glucagon increases glucose in the blood, the insulin decreases glucose in the blood and the somatostatin regulates these two functions. (15)

This is all about the sweetness in life. When the sweetness in your life is all messed up, the sweetness in your body is all messed up. Life really is all about metaphor.

ego
shadow
me
shade
superego
supershadow

# Capitolo Undici

Listen to "Caruso" by Lara Fabian

"So, do you think it's possible to fall in love with two people at the same time?" pondered Margaret.

Without skipping a beat, "Absolutely," answered Di.

"Oh, crap. I was hoping you would say, 'No way.'"

"Listen, love is a funny thing. Different people fulfill different needs. To me, it seems the most natural thing in the world to love more than one person. Sex, though, that's different. Once you have sex with someone, that changes everything."

"Don't I know it!"

"Ah... Which one? Or, was it...both?"

"No, no, just one. I wouldn't do both. Not at the same time. I wouldn't."

"Which one? Or do you not want to say?"

"I don't. It wouldn't feel right. They are so alike in some ways and so completely different in others. Whatever shall I do?"

"One day at a time. It's the only way, isn't it, ultimately, I mean?"

"They're both so wonderful..."

"Trust me, there are worse decisions to be made. Hard to believe, but true. What is it they always say in Italian, "Pian piano. Slowly, slowly"?

*****

Margaret was sitting in the Frari, the incredible church, one of a million incredible churches, in Venice. The light was shining through the window, the indescribable, the magnificent stained glass window. Titian's window. It dawned on her. It hit her. She and Michele and Ricky. She remembered. They'd been in a tryad before. Actually more than once. In permutations and combinations. The three of them. Over and over. This was an old story. Triangles. There was something about triangles. Trinities. And, one of those times, oh maybe more than one, had been right there, in Venice. She had had to choose between them before. It was playing out again. She wasn't sure why...but it was. Once as a courtesan, once as a glassblower's wife, once as a wise woman, once as an artist, once....and once and once.

Just like that, Margaret knew what she had to do.

*****

Margaret and Elisabetta were back dancing. By now, they were all getting to know her quite well and she them. She loved it. She did.

Suddenly, there he was in front of her, was the little teeny man, Lorenzo. He had been watching her dancing and smiling, appreciatively, as always, but hadn't asked her to dance. Not once, and, now that she thought about it, not for ages. Now suddenly he was there.

They had taken only a few steps when little Lorenzo said, "They told me not to dance with you." He continued, "That, if you fell on me, you would kill me..."

That brought on an unexpected but old familiar feeling for Margaret.

The shot to the solar plexus.

The shock of cold water. Of being laughed at. Mocked. Ridiculed. Shunned. Harassed. Whispered about. Ostracized. Taunted. Fuck.

Margaret looked up at the woman, the woman who had given her a hard time about her weight before, and the woman was laughing...laughing hard.

Margaret then did something instinctively. She held up her index finger in warning and waggled it at the woman, as they kept dancing.

But then, something else, something worse, happened.

The woman laughed harder.

And said something else to her neighbours, which, in turn, had them laughing.

Margaret's blood ran cold.

Margaret, in response, then did something that she had, perhaps never, done. She responded to the bully. She didn't really think about it. She just did it. She looked at the woman, with very serious intent. And, very deliberately and with fire in her eyes, made the symbol for shutting up, zipping it, holding her thumb and forefinger together and pulling her hand emphatically from one side of her mouth to the other. Thunder in her eyes. The woman stopped in her tracks. Margaret had had people make painful fun of her for most of her life.

Enough.

It wasn't until later than it dawned on her that it was probably - no definitely - the first time in her life - since she was eight years old - that she had actually addressed any one of her bullies directly.

Imagine - a whole life - fifty decades - fifty bloody decades of living putting up with all of it.

The fear... The terror... The embarrassment... The shame... The powerlessness... The horror... The loneliness... The profound unhappiness, the sensation of being alone in the world with no one who could do anything to help...no one to help. A Mum and Dad that had offered, but there was too much fear on her part that it would make the situation worse...much worse.

It reminded her of a friend, of colour, who had recently had garbage thrown at her as she walked along the street of their quiet, seemingly-loving community. If the projectile had hit her, it could, actually, have killed her. No little thing. Not in any way. The police had offered to get the cowards in the car to write a letter of apology but her friend had responded, "So that, that way, the next time they see me, they can run me over instead? No thanks, I don't think so."

The tragic dilemma of the person bullied.

All of Margaret's friends had experienced some version of this. Her gay friends certainly had; her friends who were members of a visible minority; her friends who had been heavy; her friends who had been very thin, very short, very tall; her friends who spoke other languages; her friends who had other religions. Almost all of her friends had been made fun of. And many of them persecuted. Persecuted. In cruel ways.

Children persecuting children. Children hating children. Children terrorizing children. Where the hell had all those children learned to hate? Well, guess what? They had learned from adults who hated. And, in turn, they were turning into adults who hate. Adults persecuting adults. Adults hating adults. Adults terrorizing adults. Adults, in turn, teaching children how to hate. Children who then taught their own children to hate.

How to stop the horrific cycle of the wounded wounding?

As Margaret finished the dance, thanked Lorenzo and went to sit down, she sought the woman's eyes. Margaret instinctively wanted to smile at her. To make some kind of peace. Perhaps, her gesture had been a little too much. And, at some level, Margaret didn't want the woman to dislike her. That sentiment was as old as the hills, as her Nana used to say.

But, to her astonishment, the woman wouldn't meet her eyes. Not a bit of it.

And, Margaret discovered, for perhaps the first time in her life, and, somewhat shockingly, surprising even herself, that she didn't really give a damn.

Not one single rat shit.

Margaret was willing to make peace, but if the woman wasn't interested, then she wasn't interested. The woman had lost her power to hurt Margaret. Unbelievable, really. Or rather, and extremely importantly, Margaret had taken back her power.

Liberation.

Of a sort...

For Margaret didn't tell a soul. Not Di, not Elisabetta, not Michele, not Ricky. The embarrassment still lingered. A life-time habit. It was a pretty rough story. But, she thought, after she reflected a while, she might confide in Mario. He would understand. In the end, Margaret did talk to Mario, but she never, never told anyone - not a single soul - what the woman had actually said. That wound was just too deep - too raw — and simply too painful to touch.

*****

In the early hours of the morning, Margaret awoke from a very deep sleep with a bang. It was as if she had just been awakened by a very loud clap. Her heart was pounding. She could hear and feel it in her head, feel it in her chest..."palpitando"...beating furiously.

For days now, Margaret had been seeing the symbol she always saw, in her mind's eye, before someone in her life died. This symbol had freakily predicted when someone was going to die. She had seen it every time just before one of their beloved pets died and she'd seen it - devastatingly - before people she loved passed into spirit.

She tried to settle down and go back to sleep. But sleep eluded her. Finally, hours later, she'd dozed off, only just, when she was awakened by the ringing phone.

"Margaret, sono io, it's me, Elisabetta. Margaret... Maurizio just phoned..."

"Oh, Elisabetta, no..." Margaret knew immediately. She knew the exact second.

"I'm afraid so. Maria died during the night. She was ready to go. She was..."

"Will you come over?" asked Margaret.

"I'm on my way...arrivo subito."

A life over.

Just like that.

Even though Margaret knew that Maria's spirit lived on and on, she also realized that there would never, ever, ever be another Maria.

Never...

We marveled over the uniqueness of snowflakes. Well, snowflakes were miraculous, but they had nothing on the preciousness of the individuality of people. It broke her heart.

Listen to "Goodbye" by the Spice Girls

# Thank God for Red Shoes

## Chapter 10 - The Me

The Me on the ego side of the equation is the equivalent of the Shade on the Shadow side.

If your shadow is brimming, it will stimulate your ego to keep up - to keep in balance. Fear requires nurturing. Sometimes it seems that fear exists so love can comfort it.

If your stimulated ego does not find fulfillment in Spirit energy, by living the life you were meant to live and following your calling in the service of others - with all its emerging levels - and having the courage to deal with your fears, the excess energy will sometimes bulge out into the Me. The Me is the home of false fulfillment, of coping mechanisms, and, potentially, of addictions.

If your ego can't make it to your Superego, you will feel the need for some kind of comforting or coping mechanisms -  to give you some semblance of temporary joy.

Feel better. Feel better. Feel fuller. Feel fulfilled. Feel recognition. Feel self-love. Feel excited. Feel grateful. Feel integrity. Feel better.

This is often translated into eating, drinking, smoking, gambling, compulsive buying, sex, drugs, even pain, making other people yell at you so you can experience your own adrenalin rush. Anything to make you feel better. An escape hatch. Feel better. Feel better. Feel comforted.

Any use of coping mechanisms is a substitute for the pleasurable feeling of self-love and self-actualization.

Coping mechanisms are a temporary form of pleasure until we get the more lasting kind - living a life on purpose and balancing love and fear.

The urge for love and recognition - self-love and self-recognition - is the urge to feel good. If our shadow - including our fears, our false beliefs, and our wacky agreements - has stifled us, our urge to feel good correspondingly gets bigger and bigger.

If we have been encouraged to forget our dreams and if we've then agreed to live smaller lives than we were intended to, it's all got nowhere to go but down into potential addictions.

You must do something to feel good. If it's not recognizing your own gifts and your own miraculous Godliness and dealing with your own issues, then it will be something else - drink, sex, gambling, television-watching, food, accumulating things - something - looking for ways to experience seratonin, adrenalin and anything else that makes you feel better.

Remember, there isn't anything intrinsically wrong with any of these things. What starts to be the problem is when there's too much reliance on any one or more sources of temporary pleasure to the exclusion of real joy - of joy in your being, of joy in your doing, of joy in your sense of purpose - of joy in simple things.

Things like the smell of your grandmother's cold cream or of toast made on a wood stove; the sound of your child's laughter or the sound of spring frogs; the taste of hot buttered toast; the reverence of the phenomenal night sky or the uncopyable pinks of a sunset; the touch of your pup's silky ears or the comfort of your flannelette sheet against your cheek; the sense that you can smell a deceased loved one's perfume or that you are completely supported by the Universe, a sensation of floating in a peaceful, warm serene lake with the delightful warmth of the sun revitalizing your every cell. Like being overwhelmed and humbled with gratitude for your very life.

The Me is associated with the mouth. Have you ever noticed how many addictive behaviours actually have something to do with the mouth, with breathing and with swallowing?

When you smoke, you pause and inhale deeply. That feels better. When you take a sip of coffee or of wine, you inhale. That feels better. When you eat something, your breathing changes. Regulates. You inhale. That feels better. Your esophagus and your trachea are very close together. Are we pumping something down one pipe while trying to pump something down the other?

And your voice. How often do you use a coping mechanism because you think you can't say what you really want to say? Because you can't use your voice. Or won't. Are you trying to stuff

it? To swallow the tears, rather than expressing
them?

Infants are comforted by nursing. Are we trying
to re-create the sensation of comfort, of
swallowing, of calming our breathing that is
associated with nurturing of the most basic kind?

We just want to feel better. Doing something
that is physiologically comforting. That makes
us feel better.

There are more nerve endings in the lips, tongue
and hands than anywhere else on the body. Why do
you suppose that is?

Listen to "Non Ti Scordar di Me"
by Piero Barone from Il Volo

Michele arrived back from his trip, very saddened to hear about the news of Maria's passing. He knew how much Margaret loved her and he was sad that she was sad. Margaret had attended the funeral with Elisabetta, Di, Sandra, Caterina and Maurizio. At one point during the mass, the priest, who had known Maria forever, well, he too, became overwhelmed with emotion, had had to clear his throat and fight back the tears. "Commosso" they said in Italian. Overwhelmed with emotion. Margaret had not gone to the cemetery, feeling she should leave the family to their privacy. It had been a very difficult day.

*****

Michele had invited Margaret and Di to dinner. The funeral had been difficult. The three of them were out for a walk. And walking in Venice was something else. Margaret and Michele had not seen one another since Monterosso, although they had those few phone conversations. He was over the moon to see her. The evening was warm. Strangely warm. There it was again - that wacky weather - everywhere it seemed.

"Veramente, Venezia è magica," said Michele. And it was. Truly, Venice was magic. It was illusion and fairy tales. It was endless reflection that left one in doubt as to which was which - the original image, the reflection, either, neither? Which one was real? Was either real? Venice was the five elements and then some. It was land and water, air and fire, ether. In every permutation and combination possible, and then in all combinations and permutations impossible as well. It was diffused light and endless water, melded together, no way to tell where one ended and the other began. It was a Byzantine tapestry redolent with rich velvets and soft taffetas; pastel silks and black and white stripes; with cinnamon and cloves interwoven. It was stones and gargoyles and mirrors. It was texture and colour; scent and sound and taste; and sensation beyond description. It was clocks and horses and church bells marking time, each its own personal time. It was built on the most human of scales. Entirely pedestrian. It was Vivaldi, and the ghetto, Tintoretto and Casanova and Caravaggio. It was the sweetest, most touching music that seeped into ones pores. It was eternal ghosts, eternal lovers, eternal play of light and dark and the myriad shades in between. It was gossamer poetry overlaying the most magnificent prose. It was an in-between place. It was a power place. It was the east, south, west, north, above, below and within. Venice was one of the ultimate metaphors.

They had had dinner, the three of them - Michele, Di, and Margaret - a really wondrous dinner, and it had been just warm enough to eat in a small outdoor restaurant by the side of a little canal, all in candlelight. They had eaten a huge bowl of steaming hot pasta, with leeks and squash, and had crisp, white wine. And then, the three of them had walked for miles, strolling and taking turns walking in single file, when they needed to, down some of the more narrow passageways. They had stopped for coffee and for a San Buca, with a coffee bean floating on the top.

It was late. For Venice at any rate, where the city seemed to close down relatively early. They were about to detour around Piazza San Marco when all of a sudden, they heard tenors. More than one. There on the back steps of the piazza, at the end opposite the Basilica, a small crowd had gathered around a group of gondoliers, on their way home after an evening's work. The tenors were singing. Singing, just for fun. They took turns, each one trying to outdo the others. Half in jest, half very seriously. Not unlike the way the Three Tenors did, when Pavarotti tried to out-warble Placido Domingo and José Carreras. All very playful...but underneath it, a sense of competition, along with the very obvious camaraderie.

Listen to "O Sole Mio (with joke)" by the Three Tenors
- Pavarotti, Domingo and Carreras

And there was Mimmo. Di hadn't seen him again since the first day they had met on the bridge.

Mimmo came up to Di.

"Do you want to go for a walk with me?"

"Yes, okay. Sure…" She wasn't going to miss out this time. Di felt a lot braver than she had a while back, when she first met Mimmo on the bridge.

"That is excellent. I know a little place that is still open. Would you like to go for a glass of Prosecco?"

"I would…"

"Yes, let's go… Would you like to join us?" Mimmo asked very politely. Di introduced everyone. Margaret and Michele begged off.

"You two have a great time," smiled Margaret, forever the cupid.

Michele looked gratefully at Margaret and said, "It is so warm, really, for this time of year. Shall we walk a little ourselves?"

Margaret was very tired. The day had taken its toll. Still, she did feel like walking. They ended up on the other side of the Accademia Bridge, sitting on the steps of Santa Maria Della Salute.

"This church is very special to us; you know…"

"Yes, yes, I do know. I have always loved it. Felt drawn to it…"

"It was built and dedicated to the Virgin Mary after the plague of 1630."

Oh, they'd been here before.... right here...the two of them.... the three of them.... In the same situation... perhaps...

"Every year, on November 21 - I am sure you already know - we build a bridge across the Gran Canale so that we may all come into La Salute, in thanks for allowing us to survive that plague," continued Michele. Margaret nodded. "Shall we go together this year?" he suggested.

"Oh, Michele, I am so sorry. I believe that I have to miss it. I can't believe that I am going to miss it. I keep missing Volto Santo, that amazing candlelit time in Lucca, too. I think I have a commitment to a book signing right then...in Siena."

"Next year, we will do it," Michele reassured her.

"I feel so funny, sitting right here. I am sure that we have done this before... right here...right on these steps..." Margaret was thinking out loud.

Michele looked at Margaret a little strangely and asked, "So you are very intuitive, are you not? A 'sensitivo', we say."

"Yes, I guess you could say that. Everyone is, I think..."

"Would you say there is such a thing as fate...as destiny?" asked Michele.

"I guess I would say 'yes' - but it seems to be a little more complicated - or maybe a little more simple...than that..." answered Margaret, thoughtfully.

"What does that mean? I'm not sure I understand."

"I'm not sure that I do either," answered Margaret. "Beads. That's what it seems like. Life seems to be like a string of beads. There are big beads and smaller beads. Graduated beads, just like pearls. The big beads are written in the stars. They have a quality unlike the others - a crispness. Like stars, they glitter - crisp and clear. Written in the stars. This is the stuff of 'What's for you can't go past you.' Destiny as jewelry. The smaller beads, well, the sky's the limit. Choose. Choose. Choose. The easy way. The hard way. The complicated way. The direct way. The fast way. The slow way. The painful way. The fun way. Choose. Mix them up. Are you going to get the picture this time, or do you need to start over in another life? The whole picture? A string of beads, strung by each individual, punctuated by the big beads of destiny. And strung with a catch at each end, turning the string into a circle. Tremendously exciting, really."

"I am still not sure I know what that means." Michele's eyebrows were knitted together. "All that I know is that I too feel like I know you. Like I have known you before, somehow. I felt this connection with you right away. Like we were picking up where we left off. How is that possible?"

"I know what you mean. It's just like that sometimes..."

"So, do you, Margaret, do you believe in destiny?"

"I do, but I am also aware of free will..." Margaret took a deep breath. "Listen, Michele, there's no easy way to say this. You and I, we need to talk about Monterosso. I think that we have just gone too fast..."

"Too fast?"

"Yes, too soon..." answered Margaret, very slowly.

"Ah..." Michele responded, understanding dawning.

"Let's just slow down... I need to sort myself out and it would be best if I weren't ending up in bed with you while I did it."

"Margaret, we can slow down, if that's what you want..."

"I do. I'm sorry, Michele. The time we spend in Monterosso, it really was magical - perfect, really. I'm not just saying that either. It was..."

"You are breaking my heart..." Michele needed a moment. "But, of course, I will do as you wish..." Actually, he needed much more than a moment.

"I don't really know what I wish. That is why I think that we should backtrack a little bit."

"Okay, Margaret, okay... Can I still kiss you?"

"Of course you can still kiss me..." Margaret responded, feeling lighter and heavier simultaneously.

Did she feel better? Or worse?

Listen to "So In Love" by k.d. Lang

*****

The book signing in Siena was amazing. Beautiful Siena, so unique, with its sloping piazza that looked like a rising sun, had turned out many, many people to meet Margaret at her book-signing event. Di and Margaret had had enough time to go into the Duomo, one of Margaret's favourite churches anywhere. Those magnificent arches. That floor, beyond description. It was yet another treasure trove. Margaret loved the Pisano pulpit, so unbelievably beautiful, and the two of them walked around and around it, marvelling. Both Di and Margaret were ecstatic and on the trip back to Venice, they were both higher than kites.

The next morning - happy to have gone to Siena, but happy to be back in Venice – Di and Margaret went to have coffee at the bar. Di had commiserated about the talk that Margaret and Michele had had. The conversation with Michele had been difficult, and Margaret really did not want to hurt him. But, and it was a really big "but", until she sorted out her feelings for both Michele and Ricky, it was better if she weren't going to bed with either one of them.

In the bar, without Maria, Maurizio was handling everything but he really was not well, and, understandably, he was not himself. Margaret was very worried about him.

Margaret glanced up from her caffè macchiato, espresso stained with steamed milk. The couple at the table next to her were reading newspapers. Something caught her eye. A photograph in the paper. What was that? Was that Ricky? Yes, she thought that it might be...

It was. It was a picture of Ricky. On a yacht, it looked like. He was reclining - on a lounge chair, it seemed, and he was bare-chested. Looking very relaxed. The photo must have been taken with a very long tele-photo lens. It didn't look at all like he was aware that he was being photographed.

And, beside him, a woman. A spectacular-looking woman. In an extremely small bikini. Beautiful. Young. And the headline, "Ricky Delvecchio e la sua compagna. Ricky Delvecchio and his companion." Vacationing off the coast of a Greek isle.

Margaret's mouth suddenly felt very dry. And her heart dropped. She read it again. There was no doubt. It was indeed him. And the woman with him was also very, very real. And they were in Greece. Not just out for the afternoon!!!!

The reality of that hit. The ramifications of that hit.

"That son of a bitch..." Margaret said, out loud, before she could catch herself. "That figlio di putana...son of a whore...!" She was furious, and hurt and disappointed and outraged. What the hell had he been playing at?

Di had a look at the photo. Margaret was thinking out loud, furious. She exploded.

All those things he had said. All lies. All of them. Some kind of game... What the hell??? How could she have fallen for all that crap? Oh, my God, what an absolute fool she had been. Naive...and stupid...and gullible. Oh, the mortification... What a horrific judge of character she had been. Horrific.

Margaret had believed Ricky. Believed all the wonderful things he had said about her. That she was intelligent. That she was beautiful. That she was like the sun. All that crap. Believed that he believed them. All of them. She shook her head in disbelief at her own stupidity...at her own gullibility. Ever since Margaret had met Ricky, she had always thought that he was too good to be true. Well, well...very tragically, perhaps she wasn't such a bad judge of character after all. Small comfort. Small comfort indeed... Maybe she was getting her answer.

Di took a deep breath. "Okay, listen to me, or better yet, listen to yourself! Okay, you're choked...I get that. Your feelings are hurt. You feel bruised. Okay. I get that. I really do. Under the circumstances... But listen, I love you and I have to say it straight. You are feeling pretty pissed at him, duped by him. But, seriously, truthfully, think about it. Have you told Ricky about Michele? Have you? Have you told Ricky about Michele at all? Have you told Ricky that you have been to bed with another man? Have you told him that you think you are falling in love with that other man? Or falling in love with Ricky himself? Have you? Seriously, have you?"

"You know I haven't. It just never seemed right..." answered Margaret, defensively, but despondently.

"I didn't think so. Okay, well, listen, how is what you've been doing any different from what he's been doing? Or at least what it looks like he's been doing? I mean, really? I'm not trying to be mean... But, really, how is it different? Okay, Ricky hasn't mentioned another person. He certainly hasn't told you he's been going to bed with somebody else. Or even that he's seeing someone else... Let alone, that he's gone away with someone on a romantic tryst, if that's what it is. But, listen, neither have you. Neither have you. You've done all those same things, with someone other than Ricky, and you have never mentioned a word of it to him? Isn't that so?"

"Yes, you know that it is...although I hate to admit it. I hate to..."

"And, on top of all that, it might not even be what it seems. Maybe that's his sister. Or his daughter..." Di tried to lighten the tone of it all, yet still support her friend.

"Ouch..."

"Sorry. Trying to insert a little levity here. Okay, that's doesn't seem probable, it's true. But, in the world of no assumptions, there's just no way to know what that picture means..."

"Arghhhh, I know. Shit, I know that you're right. It's just all that stuff he said..." Margaret was seriously wounded.

"Look, that could all have been perfectly sincere. You've probably said some pretty nice things to him too. They're no less true, just because he, or you, for that matter, might happen to like somebody else as well. Look, I understand that you're hurt. I do. I understand that. But, listen, I think you need to give him the benefit of the doubt. Not only that, but, if you can think that you might be falling in love with two people, you have to admit that maybe it's possible that he is too. It happens..."

"Uff, I feel so tired. Sad and hurt and tired. And I haven't felt that much this trip. Why does it all have to be so complicated? Why? That's rhetorical... by the way..."

"What is it you say, 'Not until everyone has gotten what they need to get...'?"

"I don't know what I would do without you. I really don't..." And then, softly, and still sadly, "He's still a bum..."


Listen to "Dark Horse" by Amanda Marshall

# Thank God for Red Shoes

## Chapter 11 - Equilibrium

If your shadow energy repository is too full and it has been prompting your ego but your ego has no more wiggle room, that energy has to go somewhere. Often it has nowhere to go but down, into your bulgy space, the Shade, the home of illness - both physical or mental - all illness.

It is your life, trying to get your attention in a bigger way.

Similarly, a stimulated ego forced unwillingly into addictions - into the Me - if left unchecked, will start also to seep - this time, sideways - into illness, into the Shade.

The coping mechanisms become part of the problem. Obesity, alcoholism, compulsive spending, sexual addiction etc. move into heart disease, depression, liver problems, sexually transmitted disease, suicidal thoughts, etc.

We call all of this stress. It is "negative" energy trying to get you to stop, reflect and change - whether it's a cold, diabetes or cancer.

If you are pushed - actually, push yourself - into illness, it's the Universe warning you that you're not getting it. Sometimes, you just need a rest and won't allow yourself to take one unless you are ill. Sometimes, you need a wake-up call. Sometimes, you need a crisis. Sometimes, it is telling you that you've gone past the point of no return and you're not going to get it in this particular lifetime.

All of this fits perfectly with the ancient wisdom of Ayurvedic medicine. Addictions are seen as the response to an absence of joy in one's life. (16)

And, rather than finding it necessary to combat addictions with will power, Ayurvedic medicine suggests that as you incorporate real joy in your life, the needs for the coping mechanisms will automatically fall away. (17)

For a greater understanding of Ayurvedic medicine, see Deepak Chopra's amazing book, "Perfect Health."

Today, many of us have adopted lifestyles that keep our shadows in overload. We're in defence mode all the time.

Our coping mechanisms have become more and more inadequate to deal with the volume and severity of "negative" energies we expose ourselves to.

If your shadow's negative energies are too much for you to bear, they will stimulate your ego to be even stronger. It stimulates the desire for nurturing, for appreciation and for recognition, ultimately for self-love and self-approval, for fulfillment and the immense pleasure this gives us.

The stimulated ego wants you to do what you're destined and designed and intended to do. Any use of coping mechanisms is a substitution for the pleasurable feeling of self-actualization - of peace. Coping mechanisms are a temporary form of pleasure until we get a more lasting kind - which is - Ta da - living a life on purpose.

If you have a spiritual practice, it will greatly assist to build up the positive energy and dissipate the negative energy.

Meditation, silence, singing, praying, chanting, talking to God, listening to God, being mindful, creating things - all assist - anything that takes you to the place of "no time". Music, a power beyond belief, and walking in nature are especially good. Making something is amazing. Meditation plugs you in.

Spend time with people you like. Join a club. Find a community. We are social animals and most of us do best when we are part of a community. This can do amazing things to our sense of well-being.

Laughter is particularly strong medicine giving you a double whammy of alleviating negative energy and embellishing positive energy. Find ways to laugh.

Remember that Spirit is always talking to you as well as listening to you - hence the power of words.

What song did you just hear? What message did that movie just have? Did a sign on the road catch your eye? Did someone just say something to you that hit home?

And what are you saying about your life? Are you complaining? Spending lots of time and energy talking about what you don't want?

Of course, it helps if you are living on purpose and consciously - not unconsciously performing the same old routine. You may have some excavating of your life to do.

Being of service, helping others, and, most of all, expressing your unique gifts, talents and passions are key components. If you were to volunteer, what would it be? You are unlikely to choose something that isn't important to you and close to the real you.

If only you could find them, those elusive passions! Remember them? What did you love to do as a child? Defend and nurture them as Spirit intended you to.

Something it is imperative that you keep in mind is that evolution goes on and on.

Across the days and years, often your mission changes. One set of interests to the fore at one time of your life and one set at another time. One calling fulfilled followed by another calling.

You devote your life to your children to find it's time to be an author. You are a respected talk show host, who has been living her passions when suddenly they don't feel fulfilling anymore. Maybe it's time to be a politician.

Remember that life is a creative unfolding.

As one level of your mission becomes fulfilled or is about to be, you're urged on to the next level, climbing ever higher up the spiral of evolution. This propels you to new levels of experience with your new or newly-discovered passions and desires being revealed to you from the same Source that provides their fulfillment.

From the time you're little, your first recollection of your passions are big clues.

Someone may have encouraged you to forget them. It's time to excavate.

# Capitolo Tredici

Listen to" Daybreak" by Barry Manilow

Margaret spent the next while walking a lot, and painting and reading. She really needed time alone and went several times over to San Giorgio Maggiore, the island across from the Doge's Palace, by herself, trying to clear her head and her heart. Margaret needed to sort herself out. Seriously.

It was Sunday. She made her way to mass. Margaret really did love being in church in Italy. She just loved it. One of her parents had been Catholic... and she had gone to mass as a child. But, here, now, what she loved was the absolute sacred sensation of being with a group of people that were communicating with Spirit. The voices raised in unison throughout the mass, touched her. "Allelulia...Allelulia...Allelulia..." And the hymn, "Signore nell'alto dei cieli." It was beautiful...just beautiful. It moved her every time. It was absolutely meditative... She loved being there. Felt privileged to be there. The dogma, however, was not relevant for her. When it came to the sermon, the priest, however, this time, surprised her more than usual.

The time had flown. It was advent, the first of December, and the next week was the day of the Celebration of the Immaculate Conception. The parish priest had decided to talk exactly about that, about the immaculate conception, about the lack of sin in the conception. He talked about how the Virgin Mary had always been affiliated with the sun. Margaret paid a lot of attention to that... That was interesting, wasn't it?

And, the priest went on, that one never, but never, saw an image of the Virgin Mary, neither old nor sick. "Never," the priest said, "because she was absolutely free of the original sin...had never danced with the devil." Actually, he talked at length about sin, and, remarkably, a great deal about the devil. Margaret paid close attention to what he was saying, although she obviously had her own thoughts about sin. The priest spoke of how the devil knew when people sinned. What's more, that the devil loved it - loved it - and knew - absolutely knew - when they didn't go to mass, when they didn't go to confession, when they didn't go to communion. And, of course, the devil was very happy when people lived together "in sin", rather than being married. The priest went on at some length about that too.

Margaret wondered how some of the congregation might be taking this. Couples living together had become extremely popular, was quickly replacing marriage and had been for quite a while. How were people taking that, what the priest was saying? She glanced around her, very respectfully, very discretely, wondering...

The priest then expressed that the Virgin Mary, who had always been associated with sunlight, was, amongst all the children and descendants of Adam, the one privileged, unique person to be removed, to be immune from the original sin. To be removed from the sex act, although the priest never said those actual words. That part was implicit.
Margaret started to cough. "Oh, shit..." she thought. "That damned throat chakra..." Whenever there was something she had to say but didn't, or couldn't, she would start to cough. Was she going to have to step out? She didn't want to, but she couldn't disturb the entire congregation. She just couldn't...

And then, the priest did something that absolutely made Margaret suddenly sit a little taller, and listen even more carefully. He recited a prayer about the Immaculate Conception. It began, "Vergine gloriosissima, io mi rallegro con Voi... Most glorious Virgin Mother, I rejoice with you, that in your immaculate conception, you have triumphed both against the ancient serpent and of also against sin."

Then, continuing, the priest said something that really hit Margaret hard. Profoundly. He was several sentences in, when the priest recited, "As you are so pure, so beautiful, so immaculate, please have compassion for me, whether a king or a sinner. And, as God extended to you the right, so that you would not fall under the original temptation, could you please give me your hand, so that I might not be led into temptation..."

It was the phrase "as God extended to you the right" that had her suddenly extremely attentive. The Virgin Mary had been given the right... And then, all of a sudden, it dawned...

Often, love was described or depicted as being on the right. God also was considered on the right. The devil, it followed, was on the left. The Italian word for left was "sinistra", yes, like sinister.

"So that you would not fall under the original temptation," the priest had continued.

Well, theoretically, thought Margaret, that meant that fear, the opposite of love, was on the left also, metaphorically at least. Fear was on the left.

Fear...

And God had given the Virgin Mary the right, so that she would not fall under the temptation of the left...

The left.

Oh, my God...

The original sin wasn't sex.

Not at all.

The original sin...why, it was...fear.

FEAR.
Automatically, Margaret's brain went to - "Oh, my God, what was the etymological root of "peccato", the Italian word for sin? Of "sin", in English? In all languages?" She had to find out. She didn't have an etymological dictionary with her, nor a smart phone. What did the regular dictionary say?

The mass ended. She walked back to the apartment hurriedly…fairly flew.

Turning the pages of the Italian-English dictionary, finding "peccato"…

She could feel the energy building. Sometimes, information came to her this way, not as if almost dictated, the way it so often came, but, rather as a riddle, something to solve. And then off she would head and, all the while, she could actually feel the excitement building, and building, as she went towards the solution to the riddle.

Into the dictionary, with a sense of anticipation, of being on the edge of discovery of something, of finding a key of some sort.

There it was. "Peccare." The first definition… "(religion) to sin." The second definition… "(figurative) to err." The third definition… "to be deficient, to lack." As in "Egli pecca in coraggio"… "He is deficient in courage."

Deficient….in….courage…

Deficient.

In.

Courage.

COURAGE!

For Margaret, this was the climax. The moment of the discovery of the answer to the riddle. The "aha", the "aaah - haaa". A God-moment of discovery. Of the absolute joy of discovery.

Deficient in courage. In other words, "He is afraid."

There it was.

Confirmation.

Original sin wasn't about sex at all. It wasn't.

It was about the lack of courage.

It was to have a "deficiency of courage"!!!

Somehow, it had all been mis-interpreted. Misunderstood, in some way.

"Oh my God..."

Margaret then grabbed the English etymological dictionary and searched for the origins of the English word, "sin". The dictionary said that the origin was unknown. But, come on, "sin" was the beginning of the Italian word, "sinistra", the word meaning "left." "Sin" was also the beginning of "sine", the Latin word for "without." And, they didn't know the origins!!!

Bloody hell. Sinning was about being fearful. Fearful!!!

The enormity of it all really hit her.

It was a lot.

The immensity of that particular insight, with all of its ramifications truly hit her.

This was the basis of a major paradigm shift.

The original sin was not about sex. Not about women.

The original "sin" was to be fearful. To be the opposite of love. To fall to the temptation of the left. Did that mean the left-brain also? Was head over heart a serious problem?

The worst thing one could do was to be afraid.

Afraid to live. Afraid to try. Afraid to fail. Afraid to love. Afraid to be authentic. Afraid to be rejected. Afraid to be ridiculed. Afraid to be wrong. Afraid to step outside one's comfort zone. Afraid to do something new.

Afraid to see things in a new way. Afraid to see things from a different point of view. Afraid of differences. Afraid to grow. Afraid to challenge. Afraid to be hurt. Afraid to make mistakes. Afraid to be without. Afraid to look stupid. Afraid to follow one's bliss.

Afraid and afraid and afraid.

Stealing our lives and robbing us of joy.

Making us live smaller lives than we deserved.

That was the biggest sin. Sinning was being deficient in courage. Sinning was being without love for and without faith in ourselves, and the godliness within us.

Millions of us believed something that had been misinterpreted. Perhaps mistranslated.

Accepted it as if it were the absolute truth.

It wasn't.

Margaret felt a little shaken...post-climax. Shaken. This did happen sometimes. She also felt a little like crying.

And, Margaret asked herself, not for the first time...why her? Why?

Listen to "This Girl is on Fire' by Alicia Keyes

# Thank God for Red Shoes

## Chapter 12 - So Now What?

Your job is to keep circulating positive energy into your ego and negative energy out of your shadow. Adjust. Adjust. Adjust. And keep moving forward. Put those ruby slippers on and go.

The body has processes for the elimination of negative energies and, in a natural setting, they deal with those energies very well on a day-to-day basis.

Negative energies assumed by the body during the course of the day are eliminated by urination and defecation, by sweating, sometimes by crying, sometimes by yelling, sometimes sneezing, always by breathing, by sleeping, by walking and other things.

The negativity we assume is stored in our body and the liver plays a very important role in detoxification of negative energy - physically and emotionally.

This is why the energy we allow to surround us and be inside us is so important. This is true for physical things and emotional things both.

We need to be mindful and aware of the energy of things.

Whom we spend time with. What we watch. What we read. What we listen to. What we say. What we clean with, both what we apply to our houses, our clothes etc. and what we apply to our bodies. What issues and thoughts we carry inside us. And, of course what we eat, what we drink, what we breathe. All of it. Not just some of it.

This beautiful, and natural, method for eliminating negative energies - toxins of all kinds, physical and emotional, asks one thing. And that one thing is that we be in balance and harmony with nature as much as possible.

When we're in harmony with nature, our shadow can work effectively. It can deal with perceived threats appropriately. The adrenalin response to perceived threats gets used - flight or fight, if and as necessary. It's self-preservation.

But, if we're seriously out of harmony with nature, which is where so many of us find ourselves today, the shadow is supersaturated by negative energies. It's overwhelmed by the sheer volume and frequency of negative energies we're bombarding it with.

Violence; additives; advertising; contaminated water; pesticide-ridden fruits and vegetables; animals pumped with hormones and antibiotics as well as the emotional toxins of inhumane conditions of life and death; endless messages that we're not good enough, not sexy enough, too old, too fat, too ugly; harmful chemicals in our cleaners; degrading song lyrics; polluted oceans; polluted air; a sedentary escapist lifestyle in a world gone mad. And on and on. People with overwhelmingly brimming shadows, hurling them at others.

So, how do we address this?

We need to live our passions, be of service and detoxify. We need to fill our ego and empty our shadow.

We need to return to many of the ways and practices of the planet's indigenous peoples. We need to treat our environment, our resources and ourselves with reverence and an understanding that everything - everything - is alive.

We need to be very aware of the energy - of the consciousness - of everything in our lives. From the shows you watch to your shampoo; from what your bedding is made of to your conversations. From what your children's toys are made of to what's in your candles. From who produces your food to what you take in from advertisers and teachers. From what you access on the internet to what you listen to to what you read.

Under natural conditions, the body is perfectly designed to deal with shadow energies.

Food makes you go to the bathroom. And, what produces efficient elimination? Roughage and water as well as fat. And, where do we find water-rich fibre and healthy fats? In fruits and vegetables, in seeds and nuts, in legumes, in whole grains. Eat pesticide and herbicide-free, eat the rainbow and eat in season and from local sources as much as possible.

Urination needs water. Clean, fresh amounts of water. Water keeps everything flushed and working efficiently...another process that eliminates toxins.

Exercise makes you feel better. It releases endorphins and the best exercise is a long walk, in nature, if you can get it. With every step, you release negative energy as your heel hits the ground and pick up positive energy as you roll across the ball of you foot onto your toes. There is nothing more important than this. Exercise makes you sweat. That too eliminates toxins of all kinds. Your sweat smells unpleasant to you because it is full of toxins. In "Mutant Message Down Under" by Marlo Morgan, the main character is surprised to find that she smells terrible, whereas the aboriginal people of the Outback don't smell at all. They are living an authentic life close to nature and any negative energies they encounter can be dealt with effectively by their beautiful bodies in sync with the natural world around them and living each day with reverence. (18) Exercise also naturally makes you want to drink water.

Cry if you need to. Our society discourages crying, especially in boys. If you're a parent, please consider not imposing this on your young men. Crying is a great way to shed negative energies.

Yelling is an automatic response to negative energies. We all need ways to express anger and frustration. Some cultures deal very well with this and some don't. A raised voice is a defense mechanism, tolerated in some cultures and not in others. Unfortunately, often we hurl this negative energy of ours at other people. We need constructive alternatives to doing this. Again, many indigenous peoples have ways of doing this. Try hurling you angry voice into a hole in the ground or down the toilet. Get creative.

The amazing Toltecs had a way of reviewing their exchanges of energy from across the day, rebalancing what they've given out and what they've taken in. Find out about their method of "stalking." (19)

In addition to helping rid ourselves of negative energies, we also need to address how to increase the amount of positive energy we subject ourselves too.

Some of this is pretty basic stuff – associate with happy, likeminded people; watch shows that entertain and educate in a supremely positive way; read uplifting stuff; surround yourself with natural materials and substances as much as possible; be an organic locavore who eats in harmony with the seasons; follow the natural rhythms of the planet as much as possible; take it easier in the winter and pay attention to the length of the natural light of the day, going to bed earlier during the dark months; use music you love to elevate your mood; spend wonderful time with your family and your beloved friends; do something for other people. Re-assess how much you really need. Would it matter tomorrow if you didn't have all the stuff? Would it matter if you didn't have the ones you love? What is really important? Have experiences instead of things. Sing. Dance. Draw. Play. Laugh. Be like an Italian. Or a Quebecois or Quebecoise. Or a native person, pre-invasion. Or countless other cultures who have a lot of things right.

Above all, be the best damn you that you can be. You are unique in all the world.

You love Barry Manilow, speaking lots of languages, dollhouses, yarn stores, public speaking, cooking for people and dogs. Or you love Metallica, photography, hot Indian food, tractors, solving problems, and sailing. Do them. Fill your days with them. If you are doing something for a living that makes you heart hurt, find a way to stop. If all the options and ways out of the situation are not palatable, pick the least offensive one. And then do it again. And again, if you have to. You have to find a way to love yourself enough to spend your time doing things you love to do. And making a living from them.

Really appreciate that you are unique in all the world. THE ONLY YOU THERE WILL EVER BE. With your talents, your interests, your potentials, your passions, your vehicle for being alive, and your unique expression in matter, live the best version of yourself you can.

Do what you want to do. It's a lot more fun. When you work at something with passion and love, time disappears. You want to be there. It lights you up.

You may have to excavate your life. Can you even recall what it is you love to do? Or has it been buried under your to-do lists? What did you love to do as a child? What are some of the first things you wanted to be when you grew up? Do they still resonate? Volunteer, if you can. If you can't, think about what it would be. It's likely to be something you're really interested in if you're willing to do it for no pay. Imagine how you would spend your day if you didn't think you needed to concern yourself with money. If you think you would like to do nothing indefinitely, think again. You're just tired. How would you enjoy spending your days? Really enjoy spending them?

Just keep moving towards it. Just like skipping down the yellow brick road, you have to keep moving forward.

It can all be a lot more simple than you think. You just have to keep moving forward, with intention and detachment. If you just sit down on the yellow bricks, how are you going to get anywhere? Or, if you just keep walking back and forth, doing the same thing you've always done, how are you going to get anything different ? Shake things up.

Put on those red shoes and go for a fantastic adventure of a walk - that astounding balancing act called a joyous life.

Live your life with great passion, with a profound sense of meaning and with deep thankfulness. Live out at the very extreme edge of your comfort zone.

Now, handling your fear, that's a big one. We're not talking about the kind of fear - the instinctive fear - the gut feeling - you have when you are physically threatened. Listen to that. Rather, what we're talking about is your comfort zone. It may still affect your gut and make you feel quite nervous. You have to live on the edge, stretching yourself - just a little bit - or maybe a lot.

Within your comfort zone, things feel pretty familiar, pretty routine - comfortable and safe, but not terribly exciting.

If you can just convince yourself to live on the outskirts of your comfort zone - just stretch from where you feel comfortable - your life can become very energizing.

Of course, do this with discrimination, with discernment. Pick what feels good but is just a little beyond the regular for you.

Go on a vacation alone, use your non-dominant hand, go out for dinner by yourself, change how you go to work, sing in public, paint a wall a wild colour, whatever it is that feels a little nerveracking to do. Why do we take all this stuff so seriously? It really isn't that big a deal. But it sure can feel like it. Learn something new - a language, a new skill, something you've always thought you couldn't do. Variety really is the spice of life. Be a risk-taker. Even if it's just in a small way. All these things operate on a continuum but they are all relevant. Start with something small, if that feels best, and just feel how great it feels to have conquered your fear. Stimulate your brain and empower yourself. These are all exercises in empowerment. Empowerment. Wow!

Procrastination is nothing but fear. Remember how great it feels when you tackle something you've been putting off? Get really great at facing the things you put off. Take a deep breath and dive in. How hard is it, really? Really?

You also need to deal with the accumulated "negative" stuff that you have held on to. This is a real detoxification process, of the physical toxins and of the emotional ones as well. Brenda Watson, a Doctor of Naturopathy and a Certified Nutrition Consultant, who has programs on PBS and a whole series of books, does an amazing job of assisting you with this. Clean up your house of toxins, clean up your body of toxins and let your liver do its incredible work.

And, of course, you have to be prepared to deal with your issues.

If you are well on your way to your new life, starring you, and you have some times when you don't feel so great, realize that you may simply be releasing some of the accumulated stuff you've been holding on to. Remember that suffering is pain, held on to. Don't worry if you have moments or days of not feeling so fantastic here and there. It's just toxin release.

Malfunctions are the chemical and physical manifestations of "negative" energies, forced to express themselves because they have not been allowed release.

Deal with your ego side and your shadow side and, "Voila!", you have balance. Balance...

The magic of life is to touch the bliss of the divine while you are still in a physical vehicle. Bliss.

# Capitolo Quattordici

Listen to "Quand On Est En Amour"
by Laurence Helle

Positano, all the Amalfi Coast, in fact, was incredible. Italian was a language of superlatives. Necessary to tack "issimo" on everything, turning every adjective into "the most." You needed those superlatives to describe everything. Lemons the size of grapefruit; and bougainvillea - the most amazing mauves and purples - spilling over window sills and balconies everywhere; quiet yet exuberant sophistication, with live jazz coming out of restaurants; brightly-coloured clothing; and, everywhere, pottery and lemons, lemons and more lemons. Carved into the side of a cliff, with crazy switchback roads and a wacky but necessary one-way system of driving on the main, curvy road.

The bus that Margaret and Di had taken suddenly stopped before reaching Positano proper and backed up - yes, backed up - onto a turn-around ledge, high above the surf and scarcely bigger than the bus itself. Vertigo. Such vertigo. They inched their way alongside the bus. Still, the full-size bus could go no further and they were being met by the shuttle bus from the hotel.

Margaret had been to Positano before, but Di hadn't. "Quite the place!" said Di, overwhelmed by the sheer natural beauty of the location of the city. "Another kind of beautiful. Yet another…" she exclaimed, surprised, yet again.

"Are you sure you don't mind if I go off with Ricky for the day tomorrow?" asked Margaret.

"I do not mind in the least. I'm looking forward to sometime in the sun on my own. Look, you need some time with him. You need to talk about all this stuff You really do... And you could use a little fun. You go have fun. Although why you deserve any more fun, I can't imagine!" she teased.

"I feel pretty nervous about it...although I am trying to live life without fear...I really am. We - he and I - have to have a weird conversation - about the women in his life. Yes, yes, and the men in mine. I'm not looking forward to it. I'm really not. But I will do it. I will. Tonight, however, you and I have to go to Bruno's for dinner," said Margaret, sounding decidedly cheerier as she changed the subject. "They are so nice, the nicest people ever, so sweet, and the food is out of this world!"

Their rooms had balconies overlooking the water. Heaven. After a nap and a shower, at about 8pm, they strolled gently uphill towards Bruno's. Somewhere, in a restaurant or club below them, someone was playing live jazz, a sexy saxophone wailing as only the saxophone could.

"Ah, Margherita. Che sorpresa!!! Ben tornata! Oh, Margaret, what a surprise! Welcome back!" All the staff came to greet her.

Margaret had first been to Bruno's a couple of years ago, and had instantly become friends with the welcoming staff of the restaurant. They had kept in touch, had exchanged e-mails. Margaret loved them and they her. Margaret and Di decided to it outside, across the street from the restaurant proper, high above the sea. The sky was magnificent. Clear. Starry.

And the food was excellent, as it always was. Amazing pasta and succulent fish, and their lovely dessert plate featuring three teeny portions of different types of chocolate pastries. And the conversation was so much fun. They had struck up a conversation with a couple from Oregon, a really wonderful couple, and they had laughed and laughed - a really lovely evening - so much fun.

It had been quite late when they had made their way down the hill, arm in arm, laughing and singing. Quite spontaneously, they had broken into a medley from "Mama Mia", one of their favourite movies. They had perfected Donna and the Dynamos, and, in fact, had performed the beginning of "Super Trooper" in the Victoria airport once, for the return, from Europe, of Victoria, one of Margaret's daughters.


Listen to "Super Trooper"
from the soundtrack of Mama Mia or by Abba

Margaret was in the Breakfast Room early on Saturday morning, when one of the staff came to tell her that Signore Delvecchio was on his way up.

In Ricky came, larger than life, as always, looking quite grand. He had the most amazing scarf, tied Italian-style around his neck.

"Let me look at you. Yes, as I thought, more beautiful than ever! Italy agrees with you, you know. Your eyes are particularly magnificent, different somehow..."

"Oh, Ricky, you never fail to charm," she laughed. "Would you like coffee?"

"What I would like..." he answered conspiratorially, "is to get you out of here, where I can kiss you properly. Really properly..."

"I'm almost ready."

"Hurry..."

As they reached the elevator, Ricky told her, "The weather is absolutely spectacular. We're going to go on my yacht."

"Your yacht?" Bloody hell. A pattern, was there?

"Yes, my yacht. But, first things first." In spite of herself, she fairly keeled. She was going to deal with this, she was. She was trying to give him the benefit of the doubt. Still, he made her weak in the knees, he really did. She'd forgotten how he could be. Self-assured. In command, but not overly so somehow. Tender. Sentimental. Poetic. Strong. All at the same time. It was pretty intoxicating stuff.

"You dazzle me, you know," he whispered, between kisses. "Solare, sei… You're like the sun. I know I've said it before but it hits me every time. Right in the stomach. Just like the sun. Necessary for life. So much light in your face, in your whole being…"

As they sailed towards Capri, Ricky stood behind her, in the sun and the wind, with his arms around her, just below her breasts. She leaned back against him. It was the most natural thing in the world. "Oh shit, how can I be feeling this way?" It was if Margaret had never seen the picture of Ricky and the woman in the newspaper. She did have to find a way to broach the subject. Had to find the right moment. The right way.

The wind felt incredible. The sea was indescribably beautiful. They docked at Anacapri, decided absolutely unanimously not to sightsee but rather, to walk, and to talk as they walked.

"Oh, I meant to tell you," said Ricky, "I saw Di in the hotel lobby and she asked me to tell you that she had just been invited by Nellie and Nick, that lovely couple you met last night at Bruno's, to have dinner tonight."

"Really? They were so sweet. We had the best time with them. So easy to be with."

"So you and I can have dinner together, if you want. Do you - want, that is?"

"That would be very nice, Ricky."

"How about right on board? Or would you rather we find a restaurant?"

"Oh, on board sounds amazing. If that's not too much trouble."

Back on board, Margaret went to freshen up. She still hadn't broached the topic, but she needed to. Procrastination was just fear. Ricky looked up from his book as she came across the stateroom towards him. An incredible smile lit up his face.

"You got quite a lot of sun....and wind. It suits you." Ricky said, admiringly. "You look like some kind of goddess, escaped from the sea......stunning. Really stunning. You always look stunning. Would you like a drink? A campari and soda?"

"Please..."

"Listen, Margherita, are you and Di doing anything tomorrow? I had an idea," Ricky continued as he handed her her drink.

"I don't think we had planned anything specific for tomorrow. But we are leaving first thing Monday morning."

"Well, how about tomorrow the three of us go to Napoli, to Naples. I especially want you to see the National Galleries of Capodimonte, the museum there. And, of course, it is Naples - we have to have pizza - the best pizza in the world!"

"That sounds like such a happiness. I'll need to ask Di, but I am pretty sure that she will just love the idea."

"Excellent. We'll check with her, and if it is okay, I will pick you up in the morning and we will make a day of it."

The yacht was unbelievable - beautifully appointed. The wonderful Italian singer, Tiziano Ferro was playing on the sound system. "Oh, I love him," said Margaret.

"Come Margherita, let's dance."

Ricky really was a superb dancer, of course, he was. Margaret had danced with Ricky many times, but she was always taken with how well he moved, how naturally he led, how much grace he displayed.

The song was "Troppo Buono, Too Good," by Tiziano Ferro. A bittersweet love song, with a quintessentially bittersweet Italian melody.

A song about half-truths, and complications, and tolerating too much for too long, and having to walk away for one's own sanity. A song about the pain of unrequited love and about effort unreciprocated. A song about the heartbreak of self-preservation.

Listen to "Troppo Buono" by Tiziano Ferro

"That song got to you, eh? You're different. You have been all day. What is it?" asked Ricky. Margaret looked pretty sad. She felt pretty guilty. The lyrics had really gotten to her.

"Am I?"

"Yes, I couldn't quite put my finger on it, but yes. There has been something all day... I noticed it right away." A pause. A long pause.

Ricky frowned slightly and, knowingly, unhappily knowingly, then asked, "Ah... It is a man, no?"

Margaret had been thinking a lot about the real meaning of eradicating fear. What it really meant in daily life. This was one of those moments. She knew it was important to feel the fear of having this conversation but doing it anyway. It wasn't as easy as it seemed. She dug deep.

"Yes. Yes, Ricky, it is about a man. But it is about a woman also..."

"What do you mean? Who is the man? Who is the woman?"

"He is a man I met in Venice. A chef. The woman is the one with you on this boat..."

"Ah... I see. That photo... You have been reading the tabloids, I see. Or was it the internet? It doesn't matter really... The woman. Listen, I met her long before I ever met you. And do we have a relationship? Yes, we do. At least, we have had. But it is not simple. None of this is. And, since I met you, it is even more complicated." Ricky took a breath and continued.

"I have not lied to you Margaret. You and I, we have just begun, although, every time I see you, and even more when I am away from you, I think that for you and me it is just the beginning of something. Something big, Margherita, colossal. I don't have words big enough to describe it. I just don't... And, this man, you have feelings for him?"

"It's complicated for me too, but, yes, I do."

"You are in love with him?"

"Oh, Ricky, I don't know. I may be. I'm very confused about it."

"Ah, that is good then...confusion is good. Listen, he loves you?"

"I don't know. Possibly."

"Is that what you want?"

"I'm not sure what I want. I'm just not sure. And what about her? Are you in love with her?

"I like her very much. I enjoy her. Yes, I love her. Am I in love with her? I'm not sure. I don't think so, if I am perfectly honest with myself... I don't know how else to answer that. I don't..."

Ricky continued, "Promise me you'll keep an open mind. I am coming to Vancouver on business next month. You'll be home by then. Will you promise me that you'll see me? Have dinner with me? Show me around?"

"Yes, Ricky, I will. You know I will. I promise."

"Listen, I know you think you are falling in love with this man - this cook - but you could fall in love with me, too. It wouldn't be so impossible, would it? Tell me it wouldn't."

"Ricky, what am I going to do with you?"

"Lots of things, I hope - some indecent, I am hoping..." he added, teasingly.

"Stop. Seriously!? What am I going to do with you?"

He gave her an especially convincing puppy-dog smile.

"Okay, yes, I'll see you. Sei incorrigibile. You're incorrigible!"

"Ha, yes, I am," he answered somewhat proudly. "We say 'tremendo'..."

"Okay, sei tremendo!"

"I like that better. I can take it a few different ways. Oh, what I would like to do to you...with you..." he added, longingly.

And Ricky added, "I know you won't hear of it right now. But I can be very determined - and patient - if I need to be... Listen, I just had an idea. Come with me, on Monday, as far as Rome. I have to be in the studio till about eight or nine Monday evening but we could go out then. For a drink, or something. Come on..." he urged. "Come on, give me that million-dollar smile... Come... Let's forget about all this for now..."

Listen to "O Sole Mio" by Il Volo

"Naples is gritty," everyone always said. That, and incessant talk about the crime, the pickpockets and such. Well, it was gritty. Literally. There was a lot of dust, of dirt. There was. And, in truth, a lot of garbage. Dirty, that's what it was. And, noisy. Really, unpleasantly noisy. Mostly because of the vespas. There must be several million of them. At the very least. It was also stunningly beautiful...stunningly. Like a little gem of a ragamuffin, a street urchin, one that hadn't had a bath, maybe ever...

"This could be one of the most incredibly beautiful cities in the world," said Margaret. "It is just spectacular."

"It is." answered Ricky. "It is..."

"It has a wild kind of energy...addictive somehow..." added Di.

"You know what it reminds me of?" asked Margaret. "It's very like New York. New York City. Kind of...the best and the worst of everything. And incredible, luscious - ritzy, even - neighbourhoods, and then a block too far, and, oh, oh, trouble. Suddenly very seedy. Dangerous, even... And the crime, is it as bad as people say?"

"Listen, it is like any big city anywhere. There is crime, yes, certainly, but as long as you do not flash your Rolex or make a great display of your wealth, there is not much chance that something bad will happen to you. It also helps if you look like you know what you are doing, where you are going."

"And Vesuvius," added Di. "I guess I hadn't realized just how close Vesuvius was to the city itself. It's virtually on top of it. And it is immense..."

"It is, you know, and as time goes by, people forget. They just forget, or worse, ignore, and build higher and higher up the side of the mountain. One day, it will blow again and they will be sitting right on top of it. But, look at the mountain, or at least, at what is left of it. Look at the angle of the sides of the mountain and imagine them once meeting at a peak. Imagine what it looked like before it blew. A huge portion of the mountain was simply blown, or flowed, away. A huge percentage of it. Some people say that something like forty percent of the mountain disappeared."

"It's just unbelievable. I can't get over how close it is..." said Di, shaking her head.

"Another time, we will go to Pompeii, and you will see," Ricky promised.

Margaret suddenly felt very strange. Some people calling her name. Urgently. Screaming. And, then the blast of heat, and some of them started to run, while others remained still, in disbelief. The heat...and suffocating...and screaming...

"Margaret, are you all right?" asked Ricky, looking quite concerned.

"Yes, yes, I'm fine. Just some strange kind of deja-vu. That's all. It'll pass in a minute."

"Are you sure? You look quite shaken, somehow."

"No, really, I am fine."

She'd been there before, even though she had never been there. She could remember it, as if it had been yesterday. Hear it. Smell it. Taste it. Feel it. Ah, yes, she had been there before...

The National Galleries at Capodimonte staggered her. Margaret had really enjoyed studying Art History and had taken a particular interest in Renaissance Italy. In Florence, she had been to the Uffizzi many, many times, it would take a lifetime to appreciate it all. Of course, she had been to the Accademia to see Michelangelo's David. She had also been to the Bargello to see Donatello's David, so different from Michelangelo's, and a million other things. Florence was a museum itself, so much to see. Ghiberti's bronze doors. Brunelleschi's dome. Giotto's campanile, bell tower. And on and on.

But, nothing, nothing had prepared her for Capodimonte. Painting after painting, room after room, one masterpiece after another. Botticelli. Masaccio. Rafael. Titian. Caravaggio. It took her breath away. And the strangest thing was, there was no one there. No one. The place was empty.

"Oh, Ricky, I don't know what to say. It is - I don't know - it is unbelievable. Unbelievable. I am so grateful you brought us...really... But, Ricky, why is it so empty?"

They were sitting outside, under a portico, having an espresso and a cornetto at the bar in the museum. There were only a couple of other people there.

He drank his espresso all at once. That's how they did it...intravenously. "It is not always empty. Sometimes there are many tourist buses in the parking lot. But, it is Naples, not Florence, and not every visitor to Italy comes to Naples. Pity, as there is much to delight in, as you have seen."

"Yes, yes, it is magnificent. It truly is. It makes me want to cry."

"No, no... No crying. Unless it is pure joy, of course, and then, without a doubt, you must cry! That would be the perfect thing to do." Ricky was absolutely serious. He stood. "If you two exquisite ladies will excuse me a moment... And then I will, with great relish and great pleasure, buy you both the only pizza in the world worth eating." He grinned.

As Ricky disappeared around the corner, Di looked at Margaret and said with a straight face, "If you don't want him, can I have him?"

*****

187

Back to the city they went and, as Ricky had promised, they went for pizza. Ricky, as always, was welcomed with great warmth and much hugging and kissing and a flurry of language and laughter. The three of them were ushered in past the minuscule open kitchen; past the window which opened to the outside, where people were ordering pizza from the street; and then up some very steep, very narrow and twisty stairs and into a small room upstairs.

"Ladies, shall we have wine, or might you prefer a glass of beer?"

"Oh, beer please," Di and Margaret agreed. Pizza and beer. Just like in university.

One of the owners, Paolo, was looking after them himself while his brother, Mario, cooked. He was wearing his kitchen apron, stained here and there with tomato sauce, and he looked very, very proud, as he joked with Ricky. He brought them frothy beer on tap and mineral water and they placed their orders for pizza.

"Is that a picture of Bill Clinton over there? Is that who that is with Paolo?" asked Di.

"Bill Clinton? Really?" asked Margaret.

"Ah, yes..." answered Ricky, chuckling quietly to himself. "Listen, it is one of Paolo's favorite stories. No, not one of them. It is his favourite story. When Bill Clinton was a student in England, as a Rhodes' Scholar, he had come to Naples once and had eaten pizza here at Paolo's. It made an impression. Decades later, while he was the President of the United States, he made a trip to Naples, and, quite spontaneously, and to the horror of the Secret Service, no doubt, he decided he wanted to go see if he could still find Paolo's. They closed off all the streets... They came, and, of course, it was still here - it will be here forever - and so Paolo was able to have a million pictures taken with Bill. And Bill got to have his favourite pizza once again, after all those years. Those pictures are all over the pizzeria - the original is right in the kitchen, by the takeout window, so everyone can see it."

"What a great story!" said Di. "That is quite amazing."

"You can imagine how impressive that was for Paolo, to have the President of the United States come to tell him how much he had loved his pizza all those years ago. It was a very big thing...and still is. Paolo'll be telling that story proudly for the rest of his life!"

"And the pizza itself is also amazing! I can't believe that I am eating pizza in the birthplace of the pizza!" said Margaret, taking her last sip of beer.

"Not only that, my darling, but you are eating one of the original two types of pizza. One was, and still is, just crust and tomato sauce. But the other, is the Margherita, just like you, named after Queen Margherita, with tomato, mozzarella and basilico, basil – the three colours of the Italian flag - red, white and green. All these things with a million different toppings - they are not real pizza - at least not to the purists. And, when it comes to pizza, Neapolitans are purists!!! The purist of the purists, infatti, in fact."

Paolo came to offer them a complimentary drink, Limoncello or Grappa, or  whatever they wanted. He loved Ricky, you could tell. Lots of back slapping and carrying on. As Paolo brought their drinks to them, he, very quietly at first, broke into song. "Che bella cosa, na giurnata al sole..."

"Oh, he's singing 'O Sole Mio!!!'" thought a delighted Margaret. And, very quietly, she started to sing along. So, then, did Ricky. So did Di. And then, so did everyone else in the restaurant...everyone! By the time they got to the chorus, they were very loud indeed.

She was singing "O Sole Mio", in Neapolitan dialect! With a Neapolitan!! In Naples!!! With a room full of very happy Neapolitans, with one of her best friends, and with a man who was becoming very, very important to her very quickly.

How good could life get? And, what, in God's name, had she done to deserve this much happiness?

Listen to "Angels Brought Me Here" by Carrie Underwood

# Thank God for Red Shoes

## Chapter 13 - All A Big Misunderstanding

As you can see, right now, often when we use the word, "ego", we're really talking about shadow. Thought, word and deed propelled by fear.

When we think of someone with a big ego, we're actually thinking of someone with a big shadow which is propelling ego. If someone is telling us how great she or he is, it's because she or he really doesn't think so. We know that. Fundamentally.

If someone is really great, they simply don't have to tell us so. They just exude it. And, they're really humbled by it. They have fulfilled egos and are touching their superegos.

We've been trying to bash the ego into submission, damning an intrinsic part of ourselves, all in the name of looking for balance, when what we really need to address are the conditions that have allowed our shadow side and our ego side to become so out of proportion.

Remember that an overloaded shadow, covered with emotional plaque and physical toxins, does, in fact, stimulate ego - the urge to be the incredible unique you - an astounding way for the Universe to experience itself - an extraordinary way for God to experience God.

It may be this very thing that has us totally obsessed with celebrity, thinking that all that external validation is what will make our lives perfect and our hearts sing. However, you only have to read the stories of the immense pain of incredibly beautiful souls like Princess Diana, Ricky Martin, Portia deRossi and countless others to know that being your authentic self and accepting yourself the way you are is the only way to a happy life. You have to love and accept yourself exactly as you are...right now.

Everybody wants to be rich and famous, thinking that celebrities live perfect lives. Well, we should all know better by now. What we really want is what we think they have - adoration, fulfillment, abundance, a magical life... All of that is possible and, indeed probable, if we live authentic lives, and it all springs from inside us.

Humans consistently overestimate the power of money in their happiness and consistently underestimate the power of social relationship in their happiness. Isn't that wild?

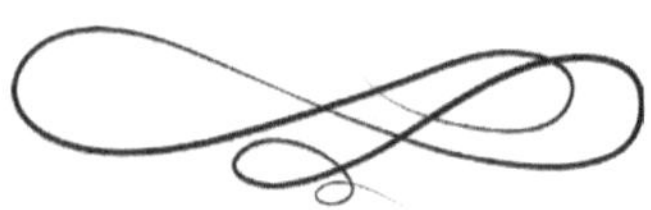

# Capitolo Seidici

Listen to "Musica Proibita" by Gianluca Ginoble from Il Volo

Ricky had booked a hotel for Margaret in Rome, and Di had continued on back to Venice. Di had a date with Mimmo that she just couldn't miss... didn't want to miss. Refused to miss.

Ricky came to pick up Margaret, as promised. They were sitting in a little bar, right in the neighbourhood of her hotel. She was nursing a glass of ruby red wine, full and delicious, and he was nursing a Scotch.

The place was full. It was somebody's birthday and there was a big party. Automatically, the people at the birthday party had invited Ricky and Margaret to join them, which they had done with great pleasure. Then, the dance music had started...all kinds of fantastic music.

"Shall we...?" as Ricky put out his hand for Margaret's.

He held her, very close, closer than he ever had. It all had a dreamlike quality.

"You and I, we are made to dance together...mmmmm..."

She felt amazing. It all felt so natural. She felt like she was home. He was dropping kisses on the top of her head.

"Allora, Margherita, do you want to dance, or do you want to...dance?" Ricky laughed as asked her, full of meaning. He was laughing at her...just a little...but it wasn't at all unpleasant.

"Oh..." answered Margaret, "I love that movie." She'd recognized that line immediately. It was from the new version of the "Thomas Crown Affair."

"There's this most incredible - cinematographically, that is - love scene." Okay, what was she doing? She was digging herself into a hole.

"Shot from above," Margaret continued, in spite of herself. "They cut it out on lots of TV channels - Pierce Brosnan's beautiful backside. His or a body double's - but I really, really hope it is his."

"Eh, you caught me! Pierce Brosnan, eh...really?" Ricky laughed at himself, but then he, after a significant pause, continued.

"So...va bene, dai...okay, come on...Margherita... Are you coming home with me?"

Margaret inhaled, but it was not a long, deep inhale.

"You know I am..." she responded.

"Grazie a Dio... Thank God..." was all Ricky said.

He took her by the hand and found a taxi.

Ricky's apartment was stunning - of course, it was - and felt just like him. Large as life; sophisticated; and incredibly comfortable, with lots of colours and textures and lots of gold. Exactly what you would expect from a Leo.

"Let's have a fire...and a nice glass of wine." Ricky suggested. "Would you like red? A glass of Montepulciano di Abruzzo? Do you know it? I enjoy it very much."

"Yes, yes, I've had it many times..." answered Margaret.

The fire felt wonderful. It was actually quite cold outside.

"Vieni qua... Come here..." Ricky said, as only he could say it.

It wasn't long before they found themselves in his very large, very comfortable bed.

"I'll make you forget the others," he whispered.

"Let's not talk about that... There's that woman, too, Ricky."

"Listen, for now..." he continued.

"Yes, for now...let's just stay right here, in the now..." Margaret agreed.

"Listen, for now...in this bed, in this room, this apartment, this city, this universe...there is only us. Just you and me. Just the two of us. All the rest will fall into place."

And, true to his word, Ricky made love to Margaret as if she were the only woman in the world.

Listen to "I Can Love You Like That" by All 4 One

*****

"Tu chi sei?....Who are you?" Ricky asked, incredulous and convinced that he was in bed with some kind of reckless angel. "Who are you? I feel like I'm with the most extraordinary woman. I feel...in paradise. I feel elated. And lighter. I feel powerful, and yet, I also feel weak. And, when you are in the throes of passion, oh my God - I can't take it. You are... esplosiva...explosive... You are killing me..." Margaret laughed. And, then, quite seriously, Ricky asked, "You will stay the night, won't you?"

"Oh, Ricky, I don't think I can... Di will..."

"Oh, Margherita, you are killing me again, a different way this time. You and I - we've only just begun. Just started. I can't let you go...not yet. Not yet. Stay. Please..."

"Okay, I'll stay, but just for a little while..."

"Excellent... You make me a happy man. Over and over. In so many ways. Teso, my darling, are you hungry?"

"Ah, I don't know... I'm too happy to be hungry." Ricky laughed, delighted by Margaret's answer.

"Ah, amore..." Ricky took her hand, kissed her knuckles, caressed her cheek with the back of his fingertips. "Shall we eat a little something...?"

"Yes, please, a little..." answered Margaret.

"I know exactly what we should have. How do you feel about eggs?"

"I love eggs."

"And truffles?" queried Ricky.

"Love 'em."

"Perfect, I'll make us some eggs with shaved truffles. Do you want to wait here - or do you want to come with me?"

"I think I'd like to come with you..." Margaret answered, with a twinkle in her eye.

"That's the girl I love - come on."

In Ricky's beautiful kitchen, he cracked eggs, the most exquisite Italian eggs, with yolks the colour of a burnished sunset - rossi, reds, they called the yolks - and whisked in the teeniest bit of cream. And, then, he shaved a black truffle over the top of the steaming creamy eggs. The man could cook. Margaret was wearing Ricky's robe, felt very comfortable with him in his kitchen, as if they had been together forever.

"Oh my God, they are perfect..." she marvelled.

"Allora, Well then..." Ricky said, with a gleam in his eye, as he put the dishes in the sink. "You know what I think...? You know that scene in 'Bull Durham', when Kevin Costner pushes everything off the kitchen table?" He was looking dangerous again.

"Oh I know it - it's some time after the 'slow, wet kisses' moment," she smiled.

"Mmmm... 'slow wet kisses'... I love that speech."

"I don't know anyone who wouldn't..."

They ended up in bed again.

Listen to "You and I" by Stevie Wonder

*****

For Margaret, that orgasm felt so different...unlike anything ever before... It rolled up... Out....

Rolling thunder...

Like...?

Like...birth.

Like birth.

That's what it was like...

Birth...

Oh... My.... God. It came to her like a stroke of lightning.

God had had an orgasm.

An orgasm.

That's what the implosion was. The "big bang". The intention...

The intention to love itself.

To love itself.

God had had a fucking orgasm...

That orgasm had created - creates - the universe and sent it rippling, expanding forever.

And, every time anyone had an orgasm - they were creating the moment of creation. They were, in fact, recreating the universe. Man, made in God's image...

And, potentially, creating more new bodies for more souls to inhabit...

"Ricky, oh Ricky..."

"Marghi, darling, are you all right?" Ricky had had his own moment.

"I have to write something down..." Margaret said to Ricky, sounding urgent.

"Okay...I'll get you pen and paper..." Thank God he understood.

That energy had ricocheted out in waves and ricocheted still. God had had a fucking orgasm in her/his desire to love herself.

And when we make love - literally, we are making...making...creating... love, we all go back and touch the rapture.

The utterly wordless, indescribable, unforgettable rapture.

Rolling thunder. From some mysterious, previously-inaccessible depth. Rolling, rolling, growing. Not unlike giving birth. Like the greatest sex. With the movement originating inside and moving out. Birth.

The birth of the universe...

The virgin birth...

Oh my God.

It all fit together.

Myths were full of stories of that which you must not do. There was more coming...much more.

Oh, God, Margaret had to get it down before it disappeared. Not disappeared... Oh...

"Ricky, I have to write. Have you got the paper, a pen? Thank you...thank you... I have to write..." Margaret started writing madly.

God had created the universe - paradise. In doing so, she/he/it - let's say Spirit – had created duality - the first fraternal twins. Light and dark, love and fear, sunlight and shadow.

And also the message...

God had said, "I have created fear, but you need not access it. There is no need.  None whatsoever. The animals will not hurt you.... Nature will not hurt you...  Nothing. They are your friends, brothers and sisters all."

But the voice of fear - that crazy, maniacal, cunning voice - had convinced them that they should eat of it.

Taste fear...

Just a taste...

One little taste...

And with that taste - that world-altering taste - they began to create hell on earth.

Fear existed...was there. It was a necessary byproduct.

But...and it was a big "but", no one had to access it.

However, fear itself had a strong, clear voice, even though compared to the love-voice of God, it was but a trifle.

But it whispered, seductively...

And so, it could be very convincing, as is fear itself...as we all know. It can convince us to negate love, deny love, falsify love...

The treachery of it.

The absolute treachery.

Margaret was writing furiously. It dawned on her. Immediately incensed her.

The gall of it...

The gall.

The unmitigated gall of bloody fear!

Paradise.

We lived in paradise.

Right now.

But, the voice of fear, the tyrant, had convinced us to eat the fruit of fear and thus to begin the decent into hell.

The original sin - fear.

Fear.

God had had an orgasm - had created dark - had created fear and its children - anger, frustration, scarcity, resentment, sadness, shame. Shame... that was the lowest of the low. God had told us - reassured us - that we didn't need to access it. No need whatsoever. Just the way a parent says, "Don't worry. It's all going to be fine..."

But the strong voice of fear itself had intervened and tempted us to access fear.

Just a little... Just one toke... One little toke.

Fear was the first drug dealer.

A low-life drug dealer.

However...

We had a choice. We had always had a choice - the gift of free will - from such a loving parent - to allow us to find our way.

It had been a virgin birth - a virgin birth - a birth arising before the existence of the two - before duality - before opposites - before male and female.

Cripes, did that make God a female...?

Good Lord, was God the Virgin Mary? Associated with the light, with the sun.

And was Jesus, beautifully and simply, steadfast and solid in his heart-knowledge that he was a child of God, as are we all?

Or, perhaps, did that make God some other concept - one we perhaps didn't have a good word for? Female and male combined - the best of both worlds, rolled into one - hermaphroditic somehow... Androgynous. Heavens, we needed a bunch of new words.

Or did that serve to confirm that God was the Great Mystery, as many, if not all, aboriginal or First Nations' People believed...forever a Mystery?

Was God awe?

Ah?

A fabulous, funny, singing, spiral-dancing, all-creative, all-loving, forgiveness-in-waiting, all-inclusive mystery?

The "ah" sound in "awe".

The "Ah" in "ah-ha" moments.

"Ah" - the sound in many of the words for God - Addio, Jehovah, Allah, Yah-weh, Buddha, Krishna, the Tao, so many others ........

And, also, the "ah" of love-making, of love, of passion - the sound often associated with climax.

The "ah" in the word "love"; the "ah" in amore...

The ramifications settled.

We live inside an orgasm, the idea of an orgasm, to be more correct.

That was fantastic...

Fantastic.

Margaret grinned.

The contrast is there. The fear that was created as a counterpoint for love. The dark that was created as a counterpoint for light. However, you don't need to access it. You can be happy.

And happier.

And then happier still.

And more creative, more imaginative, more peaceful, more joyous, more musical, more colourful, more everything...

The universe, at its origin, was a way to feel pleasure as an expression of loving oneself in the purest way.

Sex was sacred - not profane. Women were not to blame for the downfall of the entire race.

And never had been.

The two had decided together. Had eaten of fear simultaneously.

Like Disney's "The Lady and the Tramp" with a single string of spaghetti, one end of the string in each set of lips, about to meet in the middle, while the world played "That's amore."

Love and pleasure were the founding principles.

Holy shit.

"Are you okay? Your are writing like a mad woman..." Ricky really was concerned.

"It comes like that sometimes." No one had ever witnessed her writing like this before. Margaret had always been alone before.

"Are you sure you are all right? Can you tell me about it?" asked Ricky.

"Yes, yes, I'm fine - but, no, not just yet. Oh, I don't know. I feel...great...! Feel like I might want a drink."

It hit. It all hit. No more fear...not a bit of it...

NO MORE FEAR.

NO.

MORE.

FEAR.

Now she understood. She would no longer be a slave to fear, not in any way, not ever again.

Nor should anyone else...

Oh, my God...

She felt another wave. There was more...

Time was associated with fear. OF COURSE, it was. Fuck. When you did something you loved to do, you went to no time...that timeless place. If you stayed in that creative mode, in that love mode, you had the sensation of timelessness.

Shit.

The end times? They were the end of time.

The...end...of...time.

If we refused to access fear, time would disappear. We'd live forever. Life eternal. We had that, one way or another, but we'd all be aware of it in a different way. Fuck. Even the use of "fuck" made more sense. "Fuck" as an expression of delighted discovery....even that made sense...

"Marghe, are you sure you are okay...?" asked Ricky.

"Give me a minute..." Margaret needed to breathe. The impact of it all really, really hit. The ramifications.

"I can't tell if you are as white as a ghost or glowing like a lightbulb...." Ricky was more than a little concerned.

She felt....ah....oh....what did she feel?....great. She felt weird... She felt exhilarated. Exhausted. Fulfilled. Depleted. She felt overwhelmed. She felt divine.

The impact hit. The impact of what she had just been given. Margaret inhaled and held her breath a moment.

The implications on a grander scale...

The implications for the world...

"There's some more of that wine. Do you want that...or something stronger?" Ricky asked.

"Perfect. That's perfect. Ricky...?" Margaret paused, and then considering the potential enormity of it all, suggested, "Perhaps you should bring the bottle..."

"That good, eh?"

She suddenly felt like she needed to sleep but couldn't.

"Tesoro, are you sure you don't want anything else...?"

"I want you. I just want you. Love me, with all of you." Margaret started to cry.

"I am going to kiss that away - tonight and always. Do you want me to massage your back - your shoulders? Or perhaps, you'd like me to brush your hair? Do you like having your hair brushed?"

"If I didn't feel so tired, that just might be the most erotic thing you've ever said to me." Margaret looked at Ricky with - what? Relief? Joy? Gratitude, actually. He was offering to brush her hair. One of the sensations that brought her the most comfort in the world - the most peaceful sensation.

"Where is your hair brush?"

"In my bag."

In the end, Ricky brought Margaret home in a taxi very early the next morning. It was like the last scene in the "Mirror Has Two Faces", which Margaret had always loved. The one where, while they were running the credits at the end, Barbra Streisand and Jeff Bridges, so in love, were trying to find a taxi to go home and make love for the first time. Dancing and kissing and hugging and spinning, in the streets of New York City, up against car hoods, deliriously in love.

In the movie, they'd referred to how when one fell in love, truly in love, one should hear Puccini in the background. At the end of the movie, someone in a window high above the New York Street, started playing Luciano Pavarotti singing "Nessun Dorma" from Puccini's "Turandot".

But, while the credits ran, it wasn't Puccini that played. Instead, it was Bryan Adams and Barbra Streisand who were singing together underneath the scene and the rolling credits. The incomparable Barbra and Bryan Adams...Canadian, wonderful, delicious, throaty, sexy Bryan Adams.
There was light in the sky. The sun was coming up. In the streets of Rome, she could hear Brian's voice. "I've finally found someone and whatever I do it's just got to be you. My life has just begun..."

With an incredulous shake of the head, Margaret realized that her life had turned into one of her favourite movies.


Listen to "I've finally Found Someone" by Bryan Adams and Barbra Streisand

# Thank God for Red Shoes

## Chapter 14 - Something Big

No wonder you feel like you are here to do something big.

For we, who are alive on the planet now, are the generations that will stop the insanity. Stop the cycle of passing on the old habits and issues of the generation before us to the generation next to us. Stop the cycle of taking the issues of our parents, which they passed on to us and then passing them along to our children.

We're finally understanding that there's an overall design to our lives.

You've been given the perfect body, family, parents, circumstances, preferences and situations to develop your talents and to contribute to the world community as a whole. You've also been given the potential for your particular compensation mechanism - your addiction. It's given to you to keep you in physical form while you sort it out and/or so that you can have the experience of dealing with it. You can't experience the thrill of satisfaction - of a moment of illumination - those moments we love so well - if you don't have darkness to illuminate. Or, at least, that's how it seems at the moment.

You don't have the satisfaction of a job well done if there's no job to do and/or no challenge to it.

This is our evolutionary challenge - to be in
the world but not of it.

To accept duality, with all its complications,
given to us precisely to intensify the sensations
of the Universe experiencing itself.

As well, at the same time as we embrace the
blessings of duality, we really need to understand
that everything is one thing - that we are not
separate and isolated, but rather that we are,
fundamentally, the cells in the heart, body,
mind and soul of God made manifest.

Never forget that you are made of light, sound
and Spirit - that you are a bit of God.

Never forget that your psyche - your particular
shadow and beautiful ego - are to be cherished.

Your amazing body is to be loved and accepted,
exactly the way it is, honoured as an outstanding,
sensing being.

Let's all lighten up.

It's time.

# Capitolo Diciasette

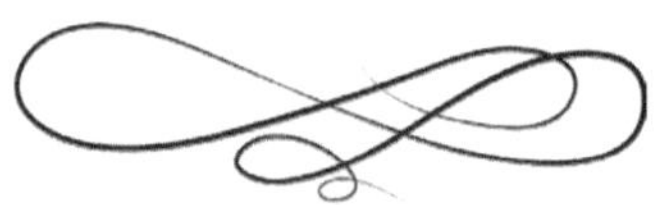

Listen to "I Believe in Us" by Amy Sky

Back in Venice, Margaret and Mario were having a drink at the bar around the corner from the dance hall.

"Okay, listen I have this favour to ask of you. I need to ask someone I trust...someone who won't laugh at me..." confided Margaret.

"What is it?" Mario was really curious

"I need a lesson in how to give amazing oral sex."

He threw his head back, laughing and laughing.

"Oh do shut up. Listen, no one I have ever been with has been interested..."

"Seriously? Are you kidding...stai scherzando?" Mario couldn't believe it.

"Seriously."

"So, you asshole, stronzo che non sei altro, will you help me out or not?"

"It will be my extreme pleasure. Shall we use props?" he laughed. "Let's see what the waiter has..."

She hit him, hard, in the arm, with the back of her hand.

*******

Firenze, Florence, really was a flower, a gorgeous, blossoming flower.

The Uffizzi Gallery, and Botticelli, and Leonardo, and the Bargello, and Michelangelo, and Brunelleschi's incomparable dome, and Ghiberti's Baptistery doors, and the Duomo, and Lorenzo de Medici and the Arno River and the Ponte Vecchio and Della Robbia's Medallions on the Ospedale degli Innocenti and ten million - at the very least - astounding experiences. Beauty and Art and Science and Literature and Language and...Margaret could expound forever.

Florence was astounding and the event there was a relatively important one. It was the only place where she was giving a full speech. What's more, she had decided to do it in Italian. Ballsy.

"Buona sera tutti. Sono contentissima di essere qui con voi stasera. Come sapete, nel mio cuore, sono Italiana. Allora, cominciamo..... Good evening everyone. I am overjoyed to be here with you tonight. As you know, in my heart I am Italian. So, let's begin..."

"We're going to talk about a lot of amazing things...a lot. And, you know what? You already know them. You already know them.

We're going to talk about a new understanding of our psyche, and then we're going to talk about how that new understanding can literally change our worlds.

At this point in our history, we're used to using the word, 'ego' as a bad word. 'Oh, he's so egotistical...', 'Oh, she's in her ego', 'That's just your ego acting up...!' We speak of it with derision, with disgust even...

First of all, does it make sense to you that we would be given an ego, a selfish, selfaggrandizing ego, one that makes us identify with things, with an inflated self-image, one that needed to be fought? Does that really resonate with you? Deep inside? Lots of people, almost everyone in fact, uses the word, "ego", that way, so it's easy to understand if you believe that definition. It's the one that's been used by the world that we know. But, does that really resonate with you? Does it?

Okay, so, what if that wasn't quite right? What if 'ego' wasn't the bad guy? Not at all. Not even one tiny bit. What, if, in fact, it's, rather, the good guy, a component in a psychological/spiritual structure - or more correctly, non-structure - one that is beautifully, exquisitely designed to keep you in balance. Balance. Equilibrium. A concept revered in the natural world.

Have you watched any of those incredible shows about the myriad forms of life on the planet? The exchange of carbon dioxide and oxygen between the plant and the animal world. The perfection of symbiotic relationships. The balance of light and dark. One side of the planet breathing in as the other side breathes out through the seasons.

Okay, so here's the model. Our new understanding of psyche has two sides. One side that is mostly about love, and the other side that is mostly about the opposite of love, that is about fear. Fear. For if you examine anger, frustration, greed, sadness, grief, depression, discouragement, and a whole bunch of other negative things, you will see that they, at their base, all spring from one thing - and that one thing is fear. Fear. Fear to be wrong, fear to be humiliated, fear to be poor, fear to be abandoned, fear to be thwarted, fear to be...you name it."

Margaret went over to reveal her chart with the diagram of the psyche on it.

"So. On one side of our new model of the psyche are all the structures having to do with fear. At the top of the column on the side of fear is the Shadow. The Shadow is an etheric pouch that handles negative energies.... anything that makes you feel scared.... that has an energy that is different enough from yours that it elicits a perceived need for protection. At the bottom of that same side is the Supershadow. It is the worst of the worst. If you have accumulated too much negative energy for your Shadow to hold, it will start to spill over down towards the Supershadow. This is the place of crime, of evil, of the "devil". Luckily for us, in the middle, between the Shadow and the Supershadow, is the Shade, a safety valve kind of place. Negative energies, if accumulated must be expressed as something. That something is dis-ease of some kind. Depression. A cold. Cancer. An accident. It's your life trying to get your attention.

On the other side, on the side of love, at the top is the Ego. An etheric pouch that handles positive energies. The urge to feel good, to feel fulfilled, to feel nurtured. At the bottom of that same love side is the Superego. It is the best of the best. If you have accumulated lots of positive energy, it will start to spill down into the Superego. This is the place of bliss, of peace, of God, of Spirit. Luckily for us, in the middle is the Me, a safety valve kind of place, between the Ego and the Superego. The urge for positive energies, if accumulated yet unfulfilled, must be expressed as something. That something is coping mechanisms - eating, drinking, shopping, thrill-seeking etc. all designed to give pleasure. It's designed to offer you temporary pleasure, while you figure out how to attain real happiness. Further, if you use the one same coping mechanism over and over, because its repeated use means you need more and more of it to give you the same perceived positive effect, that mechanism itself then becomes a problem.

And, if you continue to use temporary coping mechanisms to the exclusion of really fulfilling experiences, they too start to become a problem and often seep sideways into the Shade, creating disease.

Your job is to keep good things circulating into the system and bad things out. Those good things include love and laughter, play of the body and work of the mind, service and gratitude, following your passions, expressing unique you. Those bad things include fear and worry, inhibition and embarrassment and grudges, doing something you hate for a living, suppressing the real you.

Currently, many of us live in a world that is completely out of balance. Our Shadows are bombarded and our Egos are working hard to keep up.

And we have completely misunderstood that we are here to be happy. To have fun. It is our raison d'être.

This mode of the psyche represents duality. The love side is seen as affiliated with light and nurturing. The fear side is seen as affiliated with dark and with protection. This represents one of the first models of duality.

But there have been many messages from the universe, from God, in God's many names and faces. Many. In stories and myths from around the world. And that message is this. Fear was a necessary by-product in the creation of the world of duality, the world of experience.

However. But. Nonetheless, Regardless. Still. Comunque.

The message from God was this. Fear exists, but you need not, NOT - you absolutely need not - access it.

You live in Paradise. You have been given instinct. Instinct, you should listen to. Your gut. It will tell you when there is an earthquake coming, for instance, just the way animals now know and leave areas that are about to experience earthquakes, tsunamis and the like. Our planet is alive and changing all the time. But God was not talking about instinct. God was talking about fear. Fear. The root of all evil. Tasting fear was the first sin. The first descent towards hell.

Want a happy life?

Eradicate fear. The insidious kind. The kind that makes you afraid to try. Afraid to fail. Afraid to be laughed at. Afraid to be different. Afraid to dare to be happy. The inhibitions, the nervousness, the terror will, at first make you feel uncomfortable...no doubt.

Find a way to reframe them, repackage them. As excitement, as anticipation, as a clue that you will find true joy - TRUE JOY - in surmounting the angst.

If it has a hold over you, consider that that very charge is a real sign that it should be tackled.

And, be reassured that not too long into the experience, there comes a moment, a real moment, so powerful, when the delight of dealing with the 'danger' comes shining through. That moment when you go from hating the thought of doing it, to actually loving the experience of doing it and/ or of having done it. The moment of true empowerment. Just like in 'How To Get Naked Canada', where people who are not happy with their bodies work their way through it to a naked photo shoot.

And then, you are FREE of it... FREE!

And, then......

Then, it gets EVEN better!

On top of that, do what makes you feel like you're having fun. Do what really matters to you. For a living. For a livelihood. When you love what you do, it becomes play. Make the difference that you want to make in the world. Express unique you...unique. All your talents, all your interests, all your gifts. In a way that makes a difference in the world. In the way that you are being of service...what some people would call paying it forward. And if it's far from what you are doing now, make some kind of change that is moving towards it.

No wonder you feel like you're here to do something big. No wonder you want to be famous. No wonder. There's a very good reason why you feel these things.

For you, yes, YOU, pioneers that you are, are the generation that will stop the insanity. You are the generation that will be the first to really get it. You will be known as the generation that got it...

We live in Heaven.

In Paradise.

Right here.

Right now.

And the only thing that is stopping us from realizing that is fear, the hell generator.

Period.

Many religions, many traditions, many cultures, many belief systems understand a huge portion of this. Many. Every religion understands some of it. It's time we pieced them all together.

God is one thing and everything at the same time.

Each and every one of us is a bit of God.

And so is our planet, so are our rivers, our oceans, our animals, our plants, our mountains, our forests, our enemies....

Everything.

Sacred.

And you, you Italians, you, like many other peoples, like many other cultures...you understand, and live, a lot of this already.

You live with the seasons; you have a strong, intense sense of family; you have an astounding intrinsic way of living in community; you are open and friendly, helpful and generous; you have a strong spiritual life; you love to sing and dance, to eat and to make love; you are expressive beyond belief; you are not afraid to emote; you live with passion.

I am prejudiced, because when I am in Italy, I am 'imparadisata', Dante's word – of course, it is Dante's word - meaning to feel as if I am in Paradise. That is, quite simply, because I am. I am.

Find ways to lose your habits of fear. Those automatic little worries, those hesitations. The real sin - 'peccare' - is to be deficient...deficient in courage. That is sin.

Pleasure is not a sin. We are here, on this earth, to experience pleasure, beauty, discovery, laughter, fun, camaraderie, creativity, making love, food and drink, music, dancing and singing, and all good things.

That is why we are here. To live in Paradise. To be a fragment of God experiencing the other fragments of God; to be a piece of the Universe, experiencing the Universe...

That is why we are here.

We have play to do and work to do...a lot of it. Personal fulfillment; being true to ourselves; eradicating fear; saving our environment, our planet, which is Eden, is Heaven, quite literally; wiping out poverty and famine and injustice; stopping wars; creating solutions to the world's problems; being inspired to create, create, create.... beauty and justice and technologies and music and stories and scientific discoveries and art and a million other things, all with passion; each finding work that is fun and that contributes to all these imperative and important things.......all to create...

To create...

In the image of our creator...

Our brave new world.

We are going to do that...you...and I...and all of us...individually and together.......

Thank you...

I have enjoyed this so very much...

And may God bless us...che Dio ci benedica."

Listen to "Ti è Mai Successo" by Negramaro

# Thank God for Red Shoes

## Chapter 15 - The Wonder

We all want to feel both grounded and ecstatic, safe but with peak experiences, connected to Mother Earth and Father Sky. Walking and talking and walking our talk. We want anchors and kites.

Prem Rawat, from the events known as "Words of Peace", says that at the end of a person's life, the Egyptians used to gauge the success of a life with two questions - "Did you find peace? Did you help others find peace?" What are your answers?

Like the Tin Man, the Lion and the Scarecrow, we already have what we are searching for. We're all looking for heart, brain and courage. We just need validation - pure and simple.

And, like Dorothy, we need to find ways to love and truly accept ourselves, our lives, our circumstances, for the incredible blessings they are - even when they feel funny. This doesn't mean that we can't get better. Quite the contrary. But we have to begin with complete love and acceptance and compassion for ourselves.

We need to embrace ourselves - the good, the bad - in toto (pun intended). God bless Toto, faithful companion.

We need to count our blessings. We need to give and forgive. We need to accept our qualities and our flaws.

The ultimate recognition is that you are an extension of God - perfect in every way - exactly as you are. Today. Not in twenty pounds. Not when you stop smoking. Not when you get a nose job. Now. You can make changes that reflect that you love yourself. Stop criticizing yourself. Today. And then you'll find it easier to stop criticizing others.

Your spirit is Spirit.

And, within every living thing resides the Spirit of every other living thing.

We need to return to the wonder of life - the wonder of everything - every single thing.

The wonder.

The one who makes wonder possible.

The wonder.

Listen to "Ti Voglio Tanto Bene" by Ignazio Boschetto from Il Volo

Margaret adored Lucca. Lucca, the home of Puccini. Surrounded by foot thick medieval walls and minutes from Pisa, Lucca, like Venice, and much of Italy, was built on a human scale. And the people were wonderful.

Margaret had once had a young woman who worked in a bookstore there search forever for her to find a copy of Vasari, her beloved artist/biographer, in Italian, in a size that Margaret could carry. So sweet.

Ricky and Margaret had made arrangements to see one another there - it was close enough to Florence - and Ricky had met Margaret at the train station. He'd kissed her silly - they'd kissed one another silly - as they walked along on the beautiful boulevard and parkland on the top of the medieval walls of Lucca. They had discovered that they both loved to bicycle and had talked about renting bikes and riding on the top of the walls, something that delighted each of them beyond belief, but which they had not yet done together.

But biking be damned... Instead, Margaret and Ricky had gone immediately to their hotel room, unable to keep their hands off one another. They had had a tub together...in candlelight...bubbles everywhere.

A long while afterwards, ready for food and drink, they went for a walk, arms around each other still, stopping to have a glass of mulled wine in Piazza Napoleone. The hot wine felt fantastic...it was really cold out. It actually was threatening to snow.

They went to Margaret's favourite restaurant and had farro soup, followed by gnocci with pumpkin puree and walnuts...spectacular as always. Ricky wanted to hear all about Florence. It really had been amazing.

Ricky was dressed in midnight blue, all over, his suit, shirt and tie, all midnight blue. He looked delicious...seriously delicious.

They were just finishing with coffee.

"I just love it when we speak Italian. Aren't we lucky that we can speak to one another in a couple of languages?"

"It is, my darling."

"And isn't it particularly grand that one of them is Italian? It is the most lyrical, most amazing language. I remember loving reading 'La Bella Lingua', where I learned that although spoken 19th in world, it is the 4th most popular, most in demand from people looking to learn another language. She, the author - Diane Hales - she too has a love affair - è innamorata - with Italian."

"It's true. And translation...such difficulties with translation. The words don't mean exactly the same thing, do they, when translated from one language to another? They just don't. We've seen that again and again," said Ricky.

He took a sip of coffee and continued.

"I agree with you. Remember, Marghi, you talked about it on my show, the first time I met you. The words in one language are a reflection of that culture and its values. But, when translated into another language, itself a reflection of another distinct culture and way of looking at the world, one has to use the closest word in that other language, even though that word may not truly convey the intent of the word in the original language. So nice to be able to read literature in the original...the only way to truly get all the import..."

"I've certainly learned that, in the most visceral way, with all the stuff I learned about the word, "sin", but also throughout our - your and my - many conversations." Margaret remembered so many moments. She went on.

"John Ciardi, who did the translation of the version of Dante that I am reading describes it perfectly. He makes the point that there is a difference - worlds apart - between the feel of the word 'cute', for instance, quite short and with some hard sounds in it – and 'carina', 'cute's' Italian counterpart. It's so true isn't it? 'Carina', which is long and drawn out and ends with a vowel, as do so very many words in Italian. Softening it all. Conveying - well you know exactly what it means - sentimentality, and sweetness, and touchingly adorableness. At their core, the same, yet so different in nuance."

Margaret smiled as she added, "Ciardi also - and I remember this in great detail, for obvious reasons - talks about the similarities and the differences between the word 'daisy' and its Italian counterpart, 'margherita', or 'marguerite' in French. 'Daisy' comes from the Old English, 'day's eye', he says. And 'margherita' comes from the Greek 'margaron', which means 'pearl'. The rising sun - the day's eye - a pearl."

"Certainly connected, at one point..." said Ricky, very thoughtfully. His mind was racing.

"And, my own name, Margaret, sounds, feels and is, energetically, so different as 'Margherita'. More - I don't know - romantic, somehow..."

"They are the Romantic Languages for a good reason, no?" laughed Ricky.

"They are indeed..." agreed Margaret.

After a pause, she started a new topic, "Did you know that my friend, Mario, very, very kindly, has given me some tips on how to give really good oral sex?"

The coffee fairly flew out of his mouth. He choked...seriously, he choked. "Oh my God, Margherita, you are just..." Ricky chuckled and chuckled as he wiped himself with the still-perfect white napkin. "Just the most fantastic creature... Who else would say such a thing?" He stood up.

"Where are you going?"

"I'm taking you back to bed - right this minute. I want to know exactly - exactly – what you learned. All of it. Of course, academic curiosity, purely..." He laughed his crazy, throaty laugh. He held out his hand and gave her the greatest wink ever. "Dai Marghe, come on, let's get out of here. We have research to do..."

They were back in their room in minutes...the hotel was just around the corner from the restaurant.

"You go ahead, amore, and get into bed. I'll get us some wine...and some water. I'll be right there."

Margaret changed into a gold nightgown, long and silky. Ricky placed the wine and the water glasses on the bedside stand and got into bed with her. They were lying on their sides, face to face, each up on one elbow.

"I just want to look at you..." murmured Ricky. He was caressing her, running his fingers over her lips, the inside of her forearm. He touched her cheek, with the back of his fingertips. "Your eyes... your skin... your hair... your breasts... your unforgettable smile...you are so beautiful..."

"It is your seeing that is beautiful... You are an incredible man, Ricky. Sensitive, emotive, strong, verbal, expressive, generous of spirit, tender, masculine as hell but not afraid of your femininity..."

Making love......fare l'amore....really making love...

Ah... Ah..... Ah, my God.....

Margaret burst into tears. And, when she looked up at Ricky, he too had tears running down his face. They were both crying...

"Oh my God. I have never felt like this before. Never..." Margaret whispered.

"It's as if we were...oh, I don't know...it's as if we were angels touching God, reuniting with God. I have never experienced anything so...sacred...so... beautiful. It's the most beautiful thing I have ever felt, ever touched, ever experienced. Beyond words...senza parole..." answered Ricky. He enfolded her in his arms.

"I don't know how I lived before you..." he said as he looked straight into her eyes.

"Nor I you..." she whispered, as she looked back into his eyes, and they saw, they really saw, one another's souls.

Listen to "Cosi Celeste" by Zucchero and to "Buongiorno Bell'Anima"
by Biagio Antonacci

# Capitolo Dicianove



Christmas was approaching, although it didn't seem like it. It just wasn't as commercial in Italy as it was in North America. Di and Margaret appreciated that.

Di was packing. "How am I going to leave? How?"

"It's like that every time…I swear," answered Margaret.

"I wish we were on the same flight, at least. It's so long. And I have to go over everything that's happened again. Trying to take it all in."

"How is Mimmo taking it?"

"Oh, I don't know… The question is, how am I taking it? I got to this age, thinking that that whole romantic part of my life was virtually over…and then…"PAF", as they say here, right in the side of the head."

The doorbell rang.

"Who the hell is that?" asked Di.

The young man at the door asked for Margaret. It was just like on the show that Elisabetta and Margaret watched all the time. Hell, had somebody invited her to that show?

"A parcel for you, Signora..." the courier said, as he flashed his dimples. The Italian word for dimple was "fossetta", which kind of translated as "cute little ditch".

Translation... Inadequate translation...

Margaret tipped him and went to open the parcel.

Inside, there was a letter, a CD, and a small box, and a teeny envelope. The letter was marked 1; the CD, 2; the box, 3; and the teeny envelope, 4.

She unfolded the letter.

> *Carissima Margherita -*
>
> *Darling,*
>
> *I hope that you love the CD. I mean it.*
>
> *The box will be explained in the envelope.*
>
> *Ti adoro. I adore you.*
>
> *Ricky*

She put the CD in the player. Music. And, then Ricky's voice. He... Ricky...was singing. He was singing, Michael Buble style. He was singing... Michael Bublé's version of "All I Want for Christmas is You." Margaret burst into tears. She played it again. Di was smiling ear to ear.

Listen to "All I Want for Christmas is You" by Michael Bublé

Then she opened the box...wrapped in midnight blue, with a silver, silk bow. A bottle of perfume, it was. Unlabeled. She pulled out the topper. Oh, my God.

She opened the teeny envelope.

*Margherita -*

*Yes, my darling, it is your beloved French Lace, the original formula. It has to have a new name. I gave it one.*

*It is Cielo. Heaven.*

*Someone asked me the other day, what it was that I wanted for my children.*

*What I want for my children, for all sons and daughters everywhere, what I want for them...*

*I want them to have...*

*I want them to have...what we have.*

*Kisses on the bottom,*
*Ricky*

Listen to "Mille lune, mille onde" by Andrea Bocelli

# Capitolo Venti

Listen to "Il Cielo" by Alice

Margaret was heading home for Christmas. Time to leave. It was all mixy-uppy for her. She wanted, more than anything to be with her family for Christmas. That was what made life worth living. But she also wished she could stay in Italy. It really was home...a second home, perhaps, but a home nonetheless.

Mario had told her how much he would miss her, but added, somewhat wistfully, "It is time for you to go home and cultivate what you think you have found here." The guy was brilliant. Profoundly.

Michele had wanted to come with her to see her off, but she wouldn't let him. Ricky had also wanted to say goodbye, but she wouldn't hear of that either. Many things were calling her. Not to mention that she had work to do.

The information she had been given...well, that had the potential to change a lot of things. A lot of things... Many times, she had marvelled, and questioned and cried and felt humbled and wondered. Many times...

The one thing of which she was sure. She must eradicate fear from her life. And support others to eradicate their fears. Not instinct. That we still needed. No, it was fear that had to go. Fear, the insidious kind. Fear that made one afraid of small things, sometimes even more than of big things. A habit of worry and concern and inhibition and embarrassment...fear of making mistakes, of making incorrect choices, fear of not having enough money, fear of looking stupid, fear of being ridiculed, fear of being hurt, fear that made one procrastinate, fear of being rejected, fear of not being perfect, fear, fear, fear. Fear, robbing the potential for joy, real joy.

If the basic premise many people had been living under was in fact a misrepresentation, a misunderstanding...it was beyond Greek tragedy.

Really.

Margaret's flight was leaving very early. So early in fact, that the vaporettos wouldn't get her up to Piazzale Roma and then the airport in time for her flight. She had had to book a water taxi, one that would take her almost all the way to the airport. Elisabetta walked with her all the way to the water at San Zaccaria. It was raining, ever so slightly. They walked arm in arm, as did all best friends. Little girls, eight or eleven, or women, of literally all ages, walked, arms linked, without self-consciousness. Men didn't do it. Not yet. Still, nothing could be more natural. Very European. She had friends from England, back in Canada, who were happy to walk with her that way.

Each one of them, both Margaret and Elisabetta, with their free hand, pulled a suitcase. Margaret had been there for three months - an unbelievable, life-altering three months. The water taxi was waiting for her. The man put her luggage aboard the sleek, beautiful wooden boat. Elisabetta embraced her, one more time.

"I miss you already..." Elisabetta said it to Margaret. Margaret said it to Elisabetta. Margaret said it to Venice. Venice said it to Margaret. It rippled out across the water.

The sun was coming up. It looked remarkably like Monet's "Impression Sunrise." Crimson staining the blue...a spectacular sight.

Still it drizzled above them...her lover shedding tears as she left once more.

The water taxi sped up as they headed out into the lagoon. And Venice, la Serenissima, started to recede. Droplets of waters on the windows of the taxi, tears streaming down her face, a light mist hiding first the Doge's palace, then the Campanile, then Santa Maria della Salute, then San Giorgio...

Venice slowly disappeared behind its watery mask...

God, she loved that place.

She'd be back, she promised herself.

She'd be back...

Listen to "The Guardian" by Alanis Morrisette

# Epilogue

Listen to "Prayer" and to "L'amour existe encore" for the victims of 9/11
by Celine Dion

Put on your favourite music. Sing it out loud with glorious passion. Dance like there's no tomorrow; dance with indescribable joy, especially by yourself. Remember what it is to play.

Reflect.

What matters to you? Really matters? What is fun for you? Have you the courage to do it? What steps could you take? Today?

What difference will you make in the world? What are your gifts? How can you use them?

Today.

What would you do, if you could do anything, in your ideal world, and money were no object? What can you do to move towards it?

How can you live a life that reflects that you live in Paradise? What do you love to create? How can you protect the planet? Feed everyone? Redistribute wealth? Solve social problems? Foster acceptance? Love evil away? Protect its people? Its children? Its animals? Its plants? Its oceans and rivers and lakes? Its atmosphere? Its ecosystems? Its cultures. Its Art. Its Science. Its Awe. All of it. Each one of us plays a part. What is yours?

Then do it. Just do it. Information is not transformation. You have to take the stuff you learn and actually apply it.

Are you putting off life because you are afraid to live?

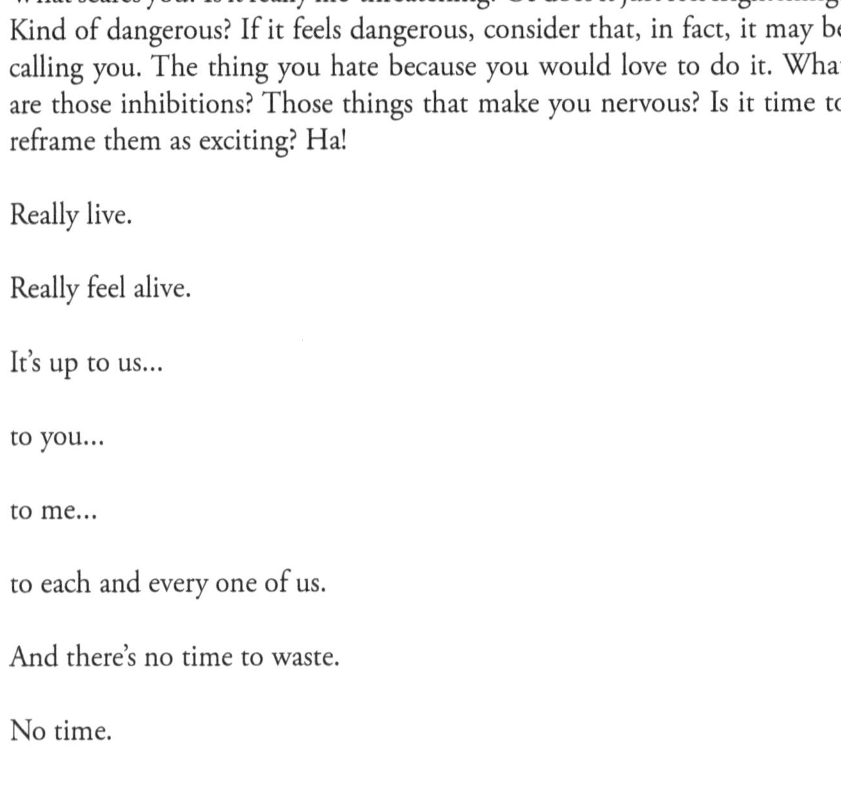

What scares you? Is it really life-threatening? Or does it just feel frightening? Kind of dangerous? If it feels dangerous, consider that, in fact, it may be calling you. The thing you hate because you would love to do it. What are those inhibitions? Those things that make you nervous? Is it time to reframe them as exciting? Ha!

Really live.

Really feel alive.

It's up to us...

to you...

to me...

to each and every one of us.

And there's no time to waste.

No time.

You get to write the epilogue...you...

Listen to "The Only Promise That Remains" by Reba and Justin Timberlake live at Oprah 2007

Listen to "Wake Up Everybody" by Harold Melvin and the Bluenotes and to "Heal the World" by Michael Jackson

The
Beginning

# Footnotes


1.  Milton, John; Paradise Lost; Penguin Classics; 2000 Wikipedia
2.  Ibid
4.  Ibid
5.  Ibid
6.  Ibid
7.  Ibid
8.  Ibid
9.  Morgan, Marlo; Mutant Message Down Under; HarperCollins; 1991
10. Wilkinson, Richard G, & Pickett, Kate; The Spirit Level; Bloomsbury; 2010
11. Weil, Andrew; Eight Weeks to Optimum Health; Alfred A. Knopf; 2006
12. Gilligan, J.; Violence: Our Deadly Epidemic and its Causes; Grosset/Putnam Books; 1996
13. Hay, Louise; You Can Heal Your Life; Hay House; 1984
14. Wikipedia
15. Ibid
16. Chopra, Deepak; Perfect Health; Three Rivers Press, Random House Inc; 2000
17. Ibid
18. Morgan, Marlo; Mutant Message Down Under; HarperCollins; 1991
19. Vigil, Dona Bernadette; The Mastery of Awareness; Inner Tradition; 2001

# Further Reading


Campbell, Joseph; Portable Jung; Penguin Books; 1976

Coelho, Paulo; The Alchemist; HarperCollins; 1998

Chopra, Deepak; Perfect Health; Three Rivers Press, Random House; 2000

Chopra, Deepak; The Book of Secrets; Harmony Books; 2004

Doidge, Norman; The Brain That Changes Itself; Viking Penguin; 2007

Freud, Sigmund; New Introductory Lectures on Psycho-Analysis; W.W. Norton; 1965

Gilligan, J.; Violence: Our Deadly Epidemic and its Causes; Grosset/ Putnam; 1996

Hay, Louise; You Can Heal Your Life; Hay House; 1984

Milton, John; Paradise Lost; Penguin Classics; 2000

Morgan, Marlo; Mutant Message Down Under; HarperCollins; 1991

Roberts, Jane; The Nature of Personal Reality; New World Library & Amber-Allen Publishing; 1994

Rowling, J.K.; Harry Potter and the Sorcerer's Stone; Scholastic Paperback; 1999

Sophocles; Oedipus Rex; Dover Thrift; 1991

Vigil, Dona Bernadette; The Mastery of Awareness; Inner Tradition; 2001

Weil, Andrew; Eight Weeks to Optimum Health; Alfred A. Knopf/ Random House Inc.; 2006

Wilkinson, Richard G. and Pickett, Kate; The Spirit Level; Bloomsbury Press; 2010

Gail Glode is a Renaissance woman - a mother, an author and motivational speaker, an artist and designer, a teacher of English as a Second Language, a linguist and a psychic. She has a B.A. from Queen's University where she studied Psychology, Italian and Art History. Gail lives part of each year on Salt Spring Island and the other part in her beloved Italy.